I0535529

The Girlfriend

Single Wide Female in Love
Book 2

By

Lillianna Blake

ISBN: 0692530053
ISBN-13: 978-0692530054

DEDICATION

To all the women out there who are new to this relationship business. Don't stop being yourself—ever.. ☺

TABLE OF CONTENTS

CHAPTER 1

The waitress cleared the dishes away from the table. I felt my heart begin to race. I gazed across the table at Max. He fumbled with his suit jacket in an attempt to smooth it down. I tried not to grin at how fussy he was about his appearance. Max always dressed well, but he never seemed to care too much about how he looked. This was the first time in a long time that I'd seen him looking even the slightest bit insecure. With a gentle touch, I reached out and straightened his lapel for him.

"Thanks." Max smiled at me. "It's nice to have you looking out for me."

A laugh bubbled up within me.

We'd been dating for exactly one year. It was hard not to think about that first kiss that we'd shared, since we were at the very same restaurant where it had happened. Max had suggested the place and the night. He had also been acting as if he had a secret.

As soon as I'd heard the plans for the evening, my

mind had gone wild with anticipation. I'd gone to a lot of trouble to be sure that my hair was perfect, my dress fit me just right, and my make-up was flawless.

Now that we'd finished our meal, I expected it to happen at any moment.

The proposal.

There was no question in my mind that Max and I belonged together. We'd talked about marriage and our future together. It was just a matter of when we would take that next step.

When Max made the arrangements for the date, I was sure that he would be taking that next step—so sure, in fact, that I'd hired a photographer to take a picture of the moment. I always thought it was a shame that most people didn't get a picture of their proposal, and I knew that it was a photograph that I would treasure.

As I waited for him to get down on one knee, my mind filled with visions of the wedding and the plans to be made.

Even though I expected it, when Max stood up my breath caught in my throat. It was hard for me to believe that it was really happening. It was everything I'd dreamed about since the very first day I met Max.

"Sammy." Max smiled.

I smiled back. Then I glanced over to where I knew the photographer was seated. The woman was poised to pounce on the opportunity.

Max continued to run his hands along his suit jacket.

"I guess you know what tonight is."

"I do." I looked up at him with adoration in my eyes. "The anniversary of our first kiss."

"That's right. It's been an absolutely amazing year—the best year of my life."

"One of many to come, I hope." My heart filled with warmth. I was dizzy with excitement. I grinned so wide that the muscles in my cheeks ached from the effort.

"Absolutely." The lights in the ceiling above him reflected in his eyes, which gave them the illusion that they twinkled. "That's why I didn't want this night to end without something special."

I gripped the edge of the table and reminded myself that no matter what, I would not trip or fall when he proposed. I wanted the moment to be perfect.

"Sammy, this is for you." He reached into the inside pocket of his suit jacket and drew out a small black box. As he held it out to me I felt my excitement deflate just a little. He wasn't on one knee. I'd expected a little bit of a speech. But I reminded myself that it didn't matter how he proposed.

"Oh, Max!" I reached out for the box. When I flipped the lid open, I felt the muscles of my cheeks finally relax. I stared with shock at the perfect heart-shaped gold charm nestled in a pillow of white. It was a stunning necklace, but it was not an engagement ring.

"Do you like it? I got it to match your tattoo." His voice was full of pride.

I jumped at the flash of the camera and Max turned toward it.

"How odd. I think that woman just took a picture of us." He shook his head. "Here, let me put it on for you." He lifted it out of the box while I still struggled to recover from my shock.

I was glad that he was occupied with the necklace. His warm fingertip swept across the sensitive skin of my neck. I didn't think that I could breathe again, but my body made me. I tried to snap myself out of my disappointment. I knew that I was being rude by not responding to him.

"It's beautiful." I willed my voice to sound genuine. I wasn't sure if I succeeded. I waved my hand at the photographer when Max wasn't looking. I didn't want her to take any more pictures. "Thank you, Max."

Max stepped back around in front of me. He leaned over to kiss me. The moment his lips touched mine it didn't matter that he hadn't proposed. I knew that he would when he was ready. My cheeks burned with embarrassment for getting myself worked up about it.

"Thank you, Sammy—for making my life so beautiful." He kissed me once more.

Really, I couldn't complain. I was amazed by Max and just how much he loved me.

CHAPTER 2

As we left the restaurant I turned back to see the photographer getting up as well. She tried to catch my attention, but I pretended not to notice. I wrapped my arm around Max's and hung on tight.

"Did you enjoy the meal?" He paused to open the car door for me.

"I did."

He reached out and repositioned the necklace. "It looks good on you."

"Thanks." I started to sit down in the car.

"Wait." He leaned close and met my eyes. "What's wrong?"

"What do you mean? We had a great night."

"Sammy, don't act like I don't know you. I can tell that you're upset."

"I'm not upset. Maybe I just ate too much." His eyes bored into mine as if he was searching for something.

"Sammy, you know you can tell me anything."

"I know."

"So tell me."

"There's nothing to tell, Max. It was an amazing meal, I love my necklace and now I'm just a little tired."

He stared at me a moment longer and then nodded.

I sat down in the car and frowned as he closed the door. It weighed heavy on my heart that he thought I was upset after he'd planned such a special night for us.

He wasn't entirely wrong about me trying to hide my feelings from him. I just couldn't shake my disappointment. I was ready to start the next chapter in our lives—our marriage—but it was clear to me that Max wasn't yet. I knew that it wasn't fair of me to try to rush him.

Just when I started to wonder what could be holding him up, he reached out and took my hand.

"I love you, Sammy."

"I love you too, Max." I leaned over to kiss him.

The passion we shared swept away the doubt in my mind. If Max needed time, that was fine with me. I knew that we belonged together.

The next morning I woke up determined to get some serious work done. I may have neglected a few days of work while preparing for the proposal that hadn't happened. It wasn't just my date with Max that had distracted me, though.

Lately, I hadn't been enjoying my apartment as much

as I once did. It had always been my retreat, my place of solace, but now it felt rather empty when I was in it. Max and I saw each other so often that it was hard for me not to feel lonely when I was at home without him.

There wasn't an inch of the place that didn't hold some memory of Max being there. So, if I made myself a cup of coffee, or picked up the remote to turn on the television, I was reminded that everything was much more fun when Max was around.

Maybe that was why I was in such a rush to get married. I looked forward to a time when Max and I would be saying goodnight rather than goodbye.

Still, as I tidied up and prepared to settle in for a writing session I felt a small pang of regret for the independence I would be losing. It was nice to be able to work in my pajamas without a thought of brushing my hair or sprucing up.

I was really passionate about my latest book in the *B.I.G. Girls Club* series. Writing on the topic of living life with confidence always helped me clear my thoughts. As I read over what I'd written already, I felt all of my anxiety beginning to subside. I'd been trying to cling too tightly to the future instead of living in the present.

I immersed myself in the book for almost two hours. When I surfaced from it, my shoulders were a little sore. I stood up and began stretching. Once I felt more limber, I reached for my phone to call Max. But then I stopped myself.

It suddenly dawned on me that I'd wrapped myself up in the expectation of being proposed to. I hadn't thought about anything else. In fact, since Max and I had begun dating, I'd spent all of my free time with him. Maybe the problem was that I'd forgotten that I had a life of my own to participate in.

Instead of calling Max, I decided to call a friend. The only problem was, I didn't have too many to choose from. I had plenty of people that were acquaintances, but very few that I considered very close friends.

It had been quite a while since I'd spoken to my friend Stephanie. Things had been tense between us for a while when she was dating Max, and we'd lost touch since then. But one thing I knew about Stephanie was that no matter what happened between us—no matter how much time passed without contact—we'd always be great friends.

I decided to give her a call. As soon as she answered she gushed into the phone.

"Oh my God, Sammy, I swear that you must be psychic."

"Huh?" I laughed.

"I was just thinking about you. I can't believe it's been over a year since we've hung out. I mean, we chat online, but when was the last time we actually saw each other in person?"

"That's why I'm calling. I wanted to see if you were available for lunch."

"Absolutely! Where do you want to meet?"

"Maria's?" I smiled. Stephanie and I always loved to binge on Mexican food.

"Okay, great. I can be there in an hour, is that okay?"

"Sure."

After I hung up the phone, I started to get excited. Stephanie hadn't seen me in a long time and I was sure she'd be surprised by the weight I'd lost. Not only that, but I would get to tell her that Max and I were dating. She and Max had dated a bit, but it never turned into anything too serious. In fact, she'd been the one to point out to me that Max and I were meant to be together.

I raided my closet for my newest outfit. It was a slingback blouse with a pair of khaki shorts. I didn't often wear shorts, but now that I felt more confident in my own body, I'd begun wearing them.

Once I was dressed I grabbed my keys and headed for the door. With a good amount of work done for the morning, I felt good about taking a short break.

CHAPTER 3

I pulled into the parking lot of the restaurant and paused to look into the mirror.

"Be mindful of what you put in your mouth," I said out loud to my reflection. "We did not work this hard to blow it all now. You still have to fit into a wedding gown."

I laughed at the thought, but really, I couldn't wait.

I walked up to the restaurant in time to see a couple step out hand in hand. I noticed that they wore wedding rings. They looked quite a bit younger than me. I had been noticing things like that lately. I didn't mean to, but I couldn't help it.

I opened the door of the restaurant. Stephanie stood up and waved to me as I walked in. We giggled as we hugged each other tight. There didn't need to be a reason for our laughter. It was just natural between us. The moment I was with her again, I was flooded with the memories of all of our past antics. I didn't know how I'd let so much time pass without seeing her.

"Wow, Samantha! You look fantastic!" Stephanie

took a step back and studied me from head to toe. "Why didn't you tell me that you'd lost so much weight?"

"Well, I still have quite a few pounds to go." I smiled. "I'm proud of how far I've come, though. You look amazing, as always."

"Thanks." Stephanie blushed a little. "I really needed to hear that."

"Of course. Is everything okay?"

We sat down together at the table.

"I already ordered some chips and salsa." She pointed to the large bowl in the middle of the table.

"Great." I snatched one up and scooped some salsa. "Now tell me what's going on?" I frowned. I could see some sadness in her expression.

"Oh, I don't want to talk about it. I want our reunion to be fun. What's been happening with you?"

I studied her for a minute. I didn't really want to let it go, but I could tell that she didn't want to talk about it just yet.

"I do have some news." I smiled.

"What is it?" Stephanie asked.

"Remember how you always used to tell me that Max and I were meant to be together?"

"Yes—because you are. You're like peanut butter and jelly—just need some bread to smash you together."

"Well I guess we found our bread." I laughed.

"What? Really?" Stephanie squealed. "That's amazing! When did this happen?"

"About a year ago." I felt a little guilty for waiting so long to tell her.

"A year? Samantha!" She looked as if she was about to lecture me, but the waitress interrupted us.

Once we'd ordered our food, Stephanie crossed her arms.

"How am I the last person to know?"

"I'm sorry. I've just been so busy. I quit my job, became a writer, had a book published…"

"Now that I knew. I read it and it's fantastic!"

"Thank you. I can't believe that you read it."

"Of course I did. Samantha, I'm proud of you for following your heart. Is there a chance of a wedding in the future?" Stephanie teased.

"I think there will be." I smiled. "I mean, we have talked about it a little."

"Oh wow. This is so exciting! I can't wait to see you as a bride. Are you going to do a big wedding or a small one?"

"Wait, wait." I laughed. "I can't think about that yet. He hasn't even proposed."

"Ah, what's he dragging his feet for? It's not like you guys haven't known each other forever."

"I honestly don't know. I keep waiting, but he doesn't seem interested just yet—and that's okay. No need to rush."

Stephanie offered a sympathetic nod. She knew me pretty well too, and I was sure that she could see the disappointment in my expression.

"Well, whenever he gets around to it, I definitely want to be there. So let me know!"

"I will of course. But what about you? We've only been talking about me. I want to know what's happening in your life." I finished the last of my burrito and sipped my water. I sat back and waited to hear all of the glorious things that Stephanie had been up to.

"Well, I'm afraid it's not as pleasant as your news. Actually, I almost got married."

"What? And you didn't tell me?"

"It was a whirlwind type of romance. You know, like the kind you read about in books or watch at the movies—girl meets boy, they fall madly in love and live happily ever after.

"That's not what happened, I take it?"

"At first it was. Dylan and I met at the grocery store, of all places, so that made it seem even more meant to be. We dated and hit it off really well. It seemed like we both wanted the same things, and honestly, Samantha, it felt as if I'd been waiting to meet him my entire life. He made me feel different than any man ever had. He was wild and spontaneous. He woke me up to the fact that life could be fun."

"So what happened?" I tried to be gentle, but I was genuinely curious. It sounded like Stephanie had met her perfect match.

"Well, he proposed. I was over the moon and of

course said yes. He wanted to go right down to a drive-through chapel and get married. As much as I admired his sense of adventure, I thought that was a little too crazy. So we moved in together first. It wasn't long before I figured out that most of his wildness came from keeping himself well lubricated."

"Huh?" I raised an eyebrow.

"I mean, he took a drink first thing in the morning. He drank on his way to work, he drank at lunch, he drank on the way home from work—it was nonstop all day. Don't get me wrong, he was never really drunk—I guess he'd developed a tolerance for it—but he always had to have something to drink."

"Wow." My eyes widened. "I can't believe that someone could live like that."

"Me either. To be honest with you, Sam, I was going to work with it. I thought—okay, we all have flaws—I'll just talk to him about his drinking and that will be that. But when I brought it up, he got really defensive. We had a horrible fight. He said things to me that I could never have imagined him saying. So, I ended it. Maybe he woke me up to the fun in life, but I wasn't about to tolerate being treated like that."

"Good for you, Steph. I mean, not that you had to go through that, but that you were able to get yourself out of it."

"It was heartbreaking." Stephanie sighed.

"Wow, I'm so sorry I wasn't there for you during that

difficult time."

CHAPTER 4

My heart ached for Stephanie. I remembered how painful it had been for me when I thought that Blue—who I now knew was Max—had rejected me.

"It's okay. I know you would have been there if I'd reached out. It was something I had to handle by myself. But now it's over and we have happy news to celebrate. You, Max, and I should get together some time."

"I would love that." A sensation of peace settled within me. I hadn't even realized how much I'd missed Stephanie's being part of my life until we were together again. "Thanks, Stephanie." I reached across the table and patted the back of her hand. "Don't let that one bad experience turn you off. Your great love is out there."

"Maybe." She shrugged. "I'm not sure that I believe in that any more."

Her words hurt my heart. I knew that she had a right to be angry, but to give up on love altogether was a depressing notion. I had been there before myself.

"Sometimes it doesn't matter if you believe in it or

not, it happens upon you anyway."

"Anything can happen, right?" Stephanie brightened. "Should we split a dessert?"

I was prepared to say no until I saw flan on the menu. "Okay, just this once." I grinned.

After we shared our dessert we walked out to the parking lot together. She paused beside her car and turned to look at me.

"Samantha, I've really missed you."

"I've missed you too. Why don't we do something together this weekend—all three of us?"

"Are you sure? I don't want to be a third wheel." She shook her head.

"I'm absolutely sure. Max would love to see you."

"Okay, great! Send me a text and let me know when and where."

"Will do!" I hugged her close. It felt good to have my girlfriend back. "I promise."

"See you soon, Samantha." She waved to me as she climbed into her car.

I walked across the parking lot to my own car. As soon as I reached it, my phone began to ring. I laughed and answered it.

"Stephanie, do you miss me already?"

"Stephanie?" Max asked.

"Oh, Max! I thought you were Stephanie."

"Okay. Why?" He laughed.

"I just had lunch with her. Can you believe it's been

over a year since I've seen her?"

"Wow, I didn't realize it had been that long."

"I invited her to do something with us this weekend."

"Us?"

I was a little surprised by his reluctant tone. "Sure, why not?"

"Well, uh, it might be a little awkward is all, since we dated."

"Max, if I had to avoid everyone you've ever dated, I'd probably have to head for Canada."

"Hey!" He laughed again. "You really think I was that much of a player, huh?"

"I'm just saying that it might be difficult." I giggled as I got into the car. "Besides, we were all friends before, we can all be friends again. Don't you think?"

"I guess you're right. If it's what you want, it's what I want."

"Oh, is that so?"

"Maybe." He sensed danger.

"I'll have to remember that."

"Oh, boy."

"Don't worry, I'll be gentle." I laughed as I hung up the phone.

Max and I had the best relationship I'd ever experienced. I never felt like I had to be a certain way to please him. There'd been none of that having to get comfortable with one another difficulty in our romantic relationship, because we were already comfortable with each other. He knew my sense of humor so well that I had to try to come up with new material.

The only thing I couldn't offer Max was a surprise.

After leaving the restaurant, I headed to the grocery store to pick up some things. As I was walking through the store, I noticed how I wasn't even drawn to the foods that I used to crave so much. Maybe it was because my life was happier or maybe it was because I had been eating a healthy diet. Either way it felt nice to march right past them.

As I loaded my grocery cart with fruits and vegetables, I noticed the man at the deli counter looking in my direction. Since I'd begun feeling more confident about how I looked, I'd recognized people noticing me more. Maybe they had before as well, and I just hadn't seen it.

I decided to ignore the attention and headed to the next aisle. I was a few aisles from the end of the store when I heard footsteps behind me. I stopped and glanced over my shoulder. It was the man from the deli counter. Now I felt a little uncomfortable. Why was he following me around?

"Are you Samantha?" he asked.

I shivered a little. I had done some online dating before things heated up between Max and me. Could this be one of the men that I'd turned down? How else would he know my name?

"Why?" I stared at him.

"I just need to know if you're Samantha."

"And if I am?"

He sighed. "Look, I'm not playing any games, I just need to know."

LILLIANNA BLAKE

CHAPTER 5

I narrowed my eyes. The man seemed rather pushy about knowing who I was. I was starting to feel very uncomfortable.

"I have Mace." I raised an eyebrow.

"No, you don't."

"What? Yes, I most certainly do and I'm not afraid to use it."

He shook his head. "I don't think you will be able to."

"Listen, I don't know who you are, or why you know my name, but I am a happily almost-engaged woman and I don't welcome your attention. So either leave me alone or I will use it."

He laughed. He actually laughed. I was stunned.

"Go ahead." He smirked.

"Okay, I will!" I reached into my basket to get my purse only to find that it wasn't there. "What?" I stared at the empty spot.

"You dropped your purse near the bananas. One of the clerks brought it to me. I thought it was you from your driver's license, but—uh—you look pretty different."

I cringed. My driver's license picture was from about fifty pounds ago. He continued, "I didn't want to tell you I had it because you could lie and say it was yours when it wasn't. You know?"

I was mortified as I processed what he'd said. In my overreacting mind, I already had him cast as a psychotic stalker looking for love.

He tilted his head toward the end of the aisle. "It's up at the deli counter, but now I'm a little afraid to give it to you. You're not going to Mace me, are you?"

"No." I frowned. "Sorry about that."

"It's alright. It's good to know how to defend yourself. I'll go get it for you."

"That's alright. I'll go with you. I need some meat anyway."

"Okay." He fell into step beside me. As we reached the counter he looked over at me. "So what exactly is almost engaged, anyway?"

"Never mind. Can I just have my purse?"

He laughed and grabbed it from behind the counter. Once he handed it over, I remembered to be polite.

"Thank you."

"No problem. Just promise me that you won't Mace me the next time you see me."

"I promise." I had no problem making that promise, as I doubted that I would ever show my face in the store again.

After I checked out I hurried to my car.

By the time I got back to my apartment I was still feeling pretty embarrassed. I tried to carry all of my grocery bags inside in one trip. I was almost to the door when I felt one of the bags get much lighter. I groaned as I realized the bag had split open. My nectarines were rolling across the floor. I dropped down onto my hands and knees and crawled after them. I grabbed one and tried to grab for another, only to grab on to a shoe instead.

"What are you doing?" Max laughed.

I looked up at him with a shy smile. "I might have had a grocery bag malfunction."

"I can see that. Here, let me help." He dropped down to the floor as well and helped me collect the wayward nectarines. "Let me help you with the rest." He grabbed a few of the bags while I collected the remnants of the broken bag.

"I didn't know you were coming over."

"I had a few minutes free and thought I'd stop by." He sighed as he put the bags on the kitchen counter. "Okay, the truth is that I missed you."

"I missed you too." I smiled and placed my hands on his chest.

He gazed into my eyes. Then we kissed. What amazed me the most after a year of dating Max—and knowing him much longer than that—was that when we kissed, it still felt just as thrilling and intoxicating as it did that first time. The kiss lingered longer than usual. When I finally broke away from him, his smile couldn't have been brighter.

"There, now I feel better." He chuckled.

"It's so nice when we get to spend extra time together." I pretended not to be hinting at anything as I put the groceries away.

"Yes, it is." He handed me the yogurt.

"I look forward to seeing you all of the time."

"Me too." He caught me around the waist and stole a quick kiss. "But right now I have to go. I really did only have a few minutes."

"Well, you arrived right on time. My grocery hero."

"Any time you need me." He kissed my forehead and then headed for the door.

I couldn't help but think about how lucky I was. Maybe I didn't have the ring yet, but I had his love, and that was all that really mattered to me.

Once I'd put all the groceries away, I looked back at my computer. I knew I had work that I could do.

After getting together with Stephanie, I thought about the way women's lives were changed when a relationship that they'd hoped for didn't go the way that they'd planned. I decided that I would incorporate that into the next chapter I was writing. It didn't matter what size you were, how old you were, or where you lived, we all had the same heartbreak when it came to a romance gone wrong.

CHAPTER 6

Over the next few days Stephanie and I texted back and forth throughout the day. We talked at least once a day. I might have used a bit of her experience as motivation for getting a few chapters under my belt. Stephanie was very open about the signs that she'd missed and how she knew better for the next time.

The mention of signs made me think that I needed to pay a little more attention to Max. Not because he might be showing signs of addiction or abusive behavior, but if there were signs for negative behavior, there had to be signs for positive behavior too. Women were bombarded with all of the things they should watch out for, but what were the good signs that should reassure them that they were in a healthy relationship?

I set up a day trip for the three of us so that Max and Stephanie could reconnect. There was a show at a botanical garden nearby that I'd always managed to miss each year. I was looking forward to having the chance to actually go this time.

I chose my favorite flowered print shirt so that I

could blend in. This wasn't just a pleasure trip, though—I took a small pen and notebook with me. I wanted to study Max and come up with a list of signs that he was a great guy—to use it for research for one of my books.

Max picked me up that morning and then we drove to Stephanie's house.

"Flowers." Max said as he turned down Stephanie's street.

"Yes?"

"Do they have food there?"

"I'm sure." I smiled.

"I hope so."

I patted his knee. "It'll be beautiful, I promise."

"I'm just saying there are lot of other things that we could be doing—like not going to a flower show."

I looked over at him. "If you don't want to go, you don't have to."

Max parked the car in Stephanie's driveway. He turned to look at me. "Sammy, I want to go anywhere that you are. Even if there are bees. Do you think there will be bees?"

I tried not to laugh, as he seemed very concerned about potential bees. "Don't worry, Max, I will protect you from any bees."

He didn't look convinced as we got out of the car. Max started to walk up to the front door. I hung back near the car.

"Are you coming?" He glanced at me.

"I'll be there in just a minute."

He looked from me to the front door and then shrugged. From the tension in his shoulders I could see that he was a little anxious. I remembered that this was likely the first time that he'd seen Stephanie since they'd broken up. As he walked up to the door, I pulled out my notebook. I jotted down a good sign.

He wants to be wherever you are, even if it's not something he enjoys.

"Hi!" Stephanie opened the door and stepped outside.

She had a big floppy hat on that made me immediately envious. I hadn't even thought of the opportunity to wear a big hat to a flower show. She paused beside Max as I caught up to him.

"Hi, Stephanie, I love your hat."

"You don't think it's too much?" She laughed. "I bought this thing to use at the beach but then haven't been to the beach since. I thought I could get some use out of it today."

"I think it's perfect. What do you think, Max?" I looked over at him.

Max's eyes widened. "I think it's—uh—it's a hat."

Stephanie and I looked at each other and laughed. I immediately felt a camaraderie with her. We looped arms and headed for the car with Max trailing behind us.

The drive to the botanical garden was all giggles and recounting past stories of things we'd done together. Max listened intently. I noticed that he looked a little surprised about some of the things that Stephanie and I had gotten into. I thought this was funny since they paled in comparison to the things Max and I had gotten into together.

"Stephanie is single, Max, so who of your friends are we going to set her up with?"

Max stared out through the windshield. "I don't know. I think Rick and his girlfriend just broke up."

"Absolutely not. No setups!" Stephanie shook her head so wildly that her hat slipped off. "I don't want any blind dates, or anything like that. If it's meant to happen, it will happen naturally."

"That's a good way to look at it." I nodded. "I promise, no setups without your permission."

"Great." Stephanie looked out the window.

I watched her expression as she stared at the passing scenery. I knew how lonely I'd once felt, despite the fact that I worked hard to be confident on my own.

CHAPTER 7

When we arrived at the gardens, I slid my arm through Max's. I was a little surprised when Stephanie hooked her arm right through Max's also. Max looked uncomfortable as he glanced at me. I smiled at him and gave his arm a little squeeze. He nodded and didn't pull away from Stephanie. The gardens were in full bloom with flowers of every color.

"Look at this!" Stephanie pointed out a huge purple flower. "Isn't it beautiful?"

"Oh yes, it is." I stared at the rich color on its petals. "Don't you think it's gorgeous, Max?" I smiled. "Max?" I turned around to see Max headed for the concession cart.

"Must be more interested in his stomach." Stephanie smiled. "I could use a drink too, actually. Do you want anything?"

"No, thanks."

I frowned as I pulled out my notebook. It wasn't like Max to not even offer to get me something as well. That certainly wasn't a good sign to jot down. But he was here when he would much rather be somewhere else, I reminded myself.

I decided to take a few minutes to watch him as if I were studying an animal in the wild. I watched as Stephanie walked up beside him. Max looked over at her and instantly smiled. She said something to him and he threw his head back and laughed. Then he reached out and touched her elbow. He leaned in close to her and whispered in her ear. Right away I wanted to know what he was whispering to her. It seemed strange to me that he had barely spoken to me, but apparently needed to confide something personal to Stephanie.

"Calm down, Sammy." I shook my head. "You're making too much out of it."

Still, it was hard for me not to notice that Max edged closer to her. Stephanie was not skinny, but she was not big either. She had a voluptuous figure that I felt many men enjoyed.

As I watched, Max and Stephanie turned to walk back toward me. I noticed that Max had two cups in his hands. My heart warmed. Here I was judging him for being friendly to my friend and not asking me if I wanted a drink, when he had taken it upon himself to get me something without asking.

"It's getting a little warm. I thought you might want some lemonade." Max smiled proudly as he offered me the drink.

"Thanks so much." I gave him a kiss on the cheek. I

still wondered what they'd been whispering about, but I told myself to let it go.

When Stephanie and Max walked ahead of me I pulled out my notebook. I added another sign to the list.

He knows what you like to eat and drink.

I didn't have to tell Max that I enjoyed a lemonade on a hot day. He knew me well enough to know what I liked.

I caught up with them at the butterfly garden. The three of us walked through the fluttering works of art together. There was something magical about the way that butterflies floated through the air. I slid my hand into Max's. He squeezed my hand and pulled me close to him.

"Alright, I guess this wasn't the worst idea." He winked at me.

I enjoyed the fact that he was willing to try something new.

We decided to have lunch at the small cafe in the garden. There was plenty of outside seating.

"I'll go grab the food, you two find a good table," I said.

"Okay." Stephanie smiled brightly. "That will give me a chance to grill Max."

"Grill him?" I raised an eyebrow.

"Oh, you know, just the normal stuff." Stephanie's eyes glowed with mischief.

I nodded, but I still wasn't sure what she meant. It wasn't as if she had to get to know Max. I was sure she already knew him pretty well. I tried to push that thought out of my mind.

I headed into the cafe to get our food. There was a window that overlooked the outside dining area. Once I ordered the food, I couldn't resist looking out the window. I saw Max pulling out a chair for Stephanie to sit in. Stephanie sat down and reached up to touch his hand in gratitude. It was an innocent gesture, I knew it was, but it made my jaw clench.

My mind flashed back to the time that Stephanie and Max were dating. Now Stephanie was single. Was it so farfetched of me to think that she might want to rekindle what they once had?

"Miss?"

I frowned as I watched Max sit down across from her. Stephanie leaned forward; so did Max. They were whispering again.

"Miss? Your food is getting cold."

"Just a minute," I snapped. I didn't normally speak to anyone like that, but I was too busy spying to get the food.

"There are other people waiting in line."

I stared as Max leaned even further across the table and whispered directly in Stephanie's ear. I was so stunned by the way it looked—his lips nearing her face— that I jerked and turned away. I turned so suddenly that I slammed right into a person who had tried to slip in front of me.

"Watch it!" He scowled at me. "It's not right for you

to make other people wait while you stalk that lovely couple."

"Excuse me?" I picked up my tray of food.

"I saw you looking at that couple out there. They're obviously in love. You shouldn't let your jealousy show so much." He shook his head and turned around to order.

His words hit me hard in the gut. I looked back out the window at Max and Stephanie. They really did look good together. I was sure that they looked better together than Max and I did. I didn't think anyone was ever going to think that Max and I were together while Stephanie was there.

I carried the tray out to the table just as the two of them were sitting back in their chairs. Max glanced up at me, slightly paler than usual, with a faint grimace. I set the tray down in the middle of the table. As they began to take their food Max looked over at me.

"Aren't you going to eat?"

"I'm not feeling up to it right now."

"Are you sick?" He frowned. "Should we head out?"

"No, I'm fine. Maybe just a little too much sun."

"Here, you should wear my hat." Stephanie smiled and plunked her big floppy hat on my head.

I felt terrible for thinking that she was being inappropriate. She was nothing but kind and generous to me. At this difficult time in her life, I knew I needed to support her, not judge her.

"Thanks."

"Thank you both for inviting me. This is the first fun day I've had in a while. I really appreciate you two letting me tag along."

"You're always welcome, Stephanie." Max offered the easy smile that had made me fall in love with him from day one.

I smiled too, but in the back of my mind I wondered what had changed. Max had been uncomfortable about Stephanie's spending time with us at first.

CHAPTER 8

After our visit to the botanical gardens, I felt strange. Part of me was elated that Stephanie was in my life again, but part of me also felt as if I was missing something between her and Max. I did my best to put it out of my mind.

The next morning I had a few hours scheduled for writing.

The upcoming section of my book was about a character that was dear to my heart. She was awkward and uncertain, just like I'd once been. I wanted to put a bit of myself into her, and see where it led. However, it was difficult for me to process my emotions and keep them separate from the character's emotions. I was so very happy, but my mind kept returning to Stephanie.

Hadn't she been convinced that she was in love? How did she go from that euphoric state to a state of utter heartbreak? I closed my eyes and took a deep breath.

Where was the calm space that I was looking for? I wanted more than anything to be able to heal that pain for Stephanie, but at the same time I couldn't fully understand it.

I hoped that I never would know that kind of heartbreak.

After losing myself in the book for a while, I heard a knock on the door. I wasn't even dressed yet, even though hours had slipped by without my noticing.

"Who is it?"

"It's me, Max."

I thought about rushing off to get pretty for him, but then I changed my mind. I was comfortable enough with Max not to worry about that.

I opened the door.

"What a nice surprise!"

"I'm glad you think so." He laughed. "I thought I should call first, but I left my phone at home."

"Oops." I grinned and kissed him. "I love it when you just drop by. As long as you don't mind my pajamas."

"Mind?" He kissed me again. "I adore your pajamas. However, if I want to take you out to lunch, you might want to change, because I'd be pretty jealous if someone else saw you in your pajamas."

"Oh, would you now?" I wiggled my eyebrows. "A surprise lunch too?"

"I figured you'd tucked yourself inside your book and had likely forgotten to eat. Am I wrong?"

"No." I shook my head. "I'll just go get changed. You're welcome to use the computer if you want to check your e-mail or anything."

"Thanks."

I ducked into my bedroom and changed as fast as I could. Max was right. I was very hungry. It amazed me how well he knew me. I reminded myself to add that to the list of good signs.

As I headed back out into the living room I saw Max hunched over my computer.

"What's this, Sammy?"

His question made my stomach lurch. In my mind I ran through all of the things he could potentially see on my computer.

"What's what?" I stepped up behind him.

On the screen was a photograph that must have been sent through while I was changing. It was from the photographer I'd hired to take pictures of the proposal that hadn't happened. The expression on my face as I looked at the necklace was horrible. It was a mixture of disappointment and anger.

"Oh—uh, nothing." I tried to reach past him to close the file.

"Wait a minute. Is this from that woman who took our picture at the restaurant the other night? I thought you said you didn't know her."

"I didn't say that exactly." Again I tried to close the picture.

Max pushed my hand firmly away from the keyboard.

"Wait just a second. Obviously you knew about it,

how else would she be able to send this to you? I thought we agreed that honesty is important in our relationship."

"Of course it's important." My heart began pounding. It wasn't often that Max's voice had that slight quiver in it. From the relaxed muscles in his face I could tell that he wasn't angry, but he wasn't pleased either. "Why would you think it wasn't?"

Max frowned as he looked back at the picture. "If you didn't like the necklace, you should have just told me."

I reached up to touch the necklace that still hung against my collarbone. "Max, I love the necklace."

"Not from this picture, it seems. Why was someone taking pictures of us?"

I opened my mouth to speak. I knew that if I told him the truth he'd understand. But I was too embarrassed to admit that I'd expected a proposal, not a necklace.

"See, you can't even tell me." He shook his head. "I don't understand why you can't just be straight with me about this."

I started to feel very defensive. The way he was speaking to me made me feel as if I was a child.

"Well, I'm not the only one keeping secrets, am I?"

"What?" Max's eyes widened. He stood up from the computer chair. "What is that supposed to mean? You think I'm keeping secrets from you?"

I'd already said it. There was no taking it back now. I realized that I had fanned the flames of a silly little spat and made it into a full-on fight. But now Max wouldn't rest until I told him what I meant.

"I'm talking about Stephanie."

"Stephanie?" Max shook his head, then stared at me. "What does she have to do with this?"

"At the garden, you two were getting pretty cozy and even whispering to each other." Even as I spoke each word I could hear how ridiculous it sounded.

Max's expression shifted from gritted teeth and narrowed eyes to a grimace. He looked away from me for a minute and then wiped his hand across his face.

"I can't believe that you would even say that to me, Sammy. Do you really believe I would do anything to hurt you, to make you doubt my love for you?" He looked back at me, and the hurt in his eyes made my heart ache. Knowing I had put it there made it even worse.

"I'm sorry, Max. I know you wouldn't do anything like that."

"Obviously you don't, if you would question me about it. You know what? Forget about lunch today. I think we both need to cool off a little while."

"Max, wait—"

"It's okay. I just think maybe we're not in the best of moods. Let's just call it a day." He turned and walked past me toward the door.

I thought of a million things I should have said, but I couldn't get my voice to work. All I could see was his back as he opened the door and walked out.

When the door closed behind him, it felt as if it struck

me right across the face. Had I really just picked a fight with Max?

CHAPTER 9

As soon as I was alone the impact of what happened knocked me right down onto the couch. It seemed to me that someone else had taken control of my mouth. The more I thought about it, the more I had no doubt that the connection between Max and Stephanie had been my imagination. I had been the one to invite them to spend the day together. I had been the one to expect a proposal and hire a photographer. It was my own guilt that had made me pounce on Max. I felt horrible.

I grabbed my phone and pulled up his number, only to remember that he told me he had forgotten his phone at home. When the voicemail came on I couldn't stop myself.

"Max, I'm so sorry. I never should have accused you of anything. I don't know what I was thinking. I can explain the photograph. Please just give me a chance."

I hung up the phone and began pacing back and forth through the living room. After I'd finally gotten everything I'd ever hoped for, in just a few minutes I might have lost all of it—all because I was jealous for no reason.

My phone began ringing. I answered it quickly—maybe Max had made it home and heard my voicemail.

"Hello? Max?"

"Sorry, no, It's Stephanie."

As soon as I heard her voice, I began to crumble. Not only had I suspected Max, but I'd suspected Stephanie as well.

"Oh, Stephanie, I did something really stupid."

"What happened? Are you okay?"

"I'm not. I'm not at all. I think Max and I just broke up."

"Wait a minute. What happened exactly?"

"Oh, I've made a big mess." I tried to catch my breath.

"Okay. That's it. I'm coming over and I'm bringing wine."

I couldn't even argue with her. I needed someone to talk to, and even though I knew she would be upset if I told her what Max and I had argued about, I still needed her.

Within a half hour Stephanie knocked on the door. I opened it to find her holding a bottle of wine and a basket of muffins.

"I wasn't sure what to bring." She frowned.

"This is perfect. Please come in." I stepped away from the door. "I can't believe that you're even here.

After what you went through without me."

"Samantha, you have to stop thinking about that. I know that if I'd picked up the phone and called you, you would have been there for me in a second. I didn't call, because there was nothing to be done. This is different."

"Is it?" I wiped at my eyes. "Do you think that something can be done?"

"Was it really that bad?"

"I don't know. I can't think straight long enough to figure it out."

"Okay, so walk me through this, because I find it hard to believe that you and Max broke up. Yesterday things seemed great."

"Well, we had a fight."

"A fight?" Stephanie smiled. "That's not breaking up, sweetie. Is this your first one?"

"I guess." I frowned. "I did something terrible. I accused him of being untrustworthy." I poured us each a glass of wine.

Stephanie took her glass and shook her head. "Oh my god, you can't be serious."

"I know! Max is the most trustworthy—"

"He has literally dated half of the available women in the city."

"Wait, what?" My breath caught in my throat.

"Listen, I'm just saying that you have every reason to doubt him. He's a ladies' man and that's a hard reputation to shake."

"But I don't." I groaned and flopped down on the couch.

Stephanie sat down beside me.

I looked over at her, my eyes filling with tears. "I don't doubt him at all. I trust Max. That isn't the problem."

"Then I don't understand." Stephanie frowned. "You said that you fought with him because you suspected him of something."

"Yes, but I only suspected him of it because of me."

Stephanie took a big swallow of her wine. "I think that you're going to have to explain this to me."

"Okay." I took a deep breath. "I need to talk it out anyway. The truth is, when Max took me to dinner the other night, I thought he was going to propose."

"Oh." Stephanie nodded. "That makes sense."

"I thought it did. We were back at the same restaurant where we shared our first kiss as a couple. It was our one-year anniversary. I had every reason to think it, right? I mean, I'm not crazy?"

"Not crazy at all. That sounds like the perfect setup for a proposal. Maybe he got too nervous to ask?"

"Not at all! He had a little black box for me, but inside was this!" I held out the heart charm. "Isn't it beautiful?"

"Yes, it's gorgeous."

"Right? But it's *not* an engagement ring. I thought it was going to be an engagement ring. So even though it's a gorgeous necklace—and thoughtful and everything—I was a little disappointed."

"Honey, of course you were."

"But then I started to think about why it wasn't an engagement ring. It's not as if Max and I need to get to know each other. So what was he waiting for? Then of course I began to ask myself, why would Max even want to be with me? I started going a little crazy. I even thought he was trying to—" I winced and looked over at her. "Get back together with you."

"Oh, Samantha!" Stephanie set her glass down hard on the coffee table. "That's not happening!"

"I know that now, but I just got crazy about it. Then Max walked out the door."

"What did he say exactly?"

"He said that we both needed to calm down and that we should call it a day."

"That doesn't sound like a break-up to me." Stephanie shook her head. "Did I ever tell you I once tried to pick a fight with Max?"

"What?" I looked at her nervously. I didn't really want to hear about the time that they were together.

"Well, here's the thing. I'm a very physical person. From the way Max acted, I thought he would be too."

"Physical?"

"Sexual."

"Oh, no, no, nope—don't want to hear about that." I plucked my wine glass from the table and refilled it as I stood up.

"Wait, it's not what you think."

"Stephanie, I adore you, but I don't see how reliving your intimate moments with Max is going to help me feel better."

"Trust me, just hear me out. It'll be worth it."

CHAPTER 10

I nearly choked on my swallow of wine. My mind spun with the buzz of alcohol and hot jealousy. I didn't want to know anything about Stephanie and Max's bedroom habits. Before I could protest she continued.

"I kept coming on to him—and Max—he would flirt a bit, be a little playful—"

"Oh, seriously, Stephanie—" I clasped my hand over my mouth to keep my wine down.

"But he never let it get very far. I was getting really irritated. Other men I'd been with would get all hot and bothered when we argued, like somehow the fight would get their engines revved."

"Still not enjoying this." I cringed.

"Anyway, I decided to poke the bear. I tried to get him into an argument. I really turned up the nag factor. I demanded his attention, pushing his buttons until I expected that he'd explode. Just when I thought I had him at his boiling point, he just looked at me, and this— oh my god—this is what he said..." She paused and took a deep breath. She raised her shoulders up and deepened her voice. "Stephanie, I respect you and I want you to respect me. So I'm just going to leave. We both need to calm down. Then we can talk about this."

"Wow." I blinked, as that was not what I was expecting. "Did he really leave?"

"Yes. He walked out, cool as a cucumber. Then the next day he showed up, sat me down, and told me flat out that what he offered was all he could offer. He wanted to take things slow."

I stared at her for a long moment. "Wait, are you saying that you and he never—"

"Not even close." Stephanie laughed. "To be honest, I got tired of waiting."

"But Max is so sensual." I shook my head.

"Maybe he is with you, Samantha—maybe he is when he's with the person that he's meant to be with. Maybe that was the problem. It's not like he just fell in love with you, you know."

I sat back at her words. It was the first time I really wondered how long Max had known that he was in love with me. I had been pining for him for years, but had he been in love with me too?

"I can't believe it. I never would have thought he was holding back."

"It wasn't just with me either. I know a few of the girls he dated after me, and they all had the same complaint. One even tried to sneak him a Viagra."

Stephanie broke down giggling.

I had to join in. I wasn't just laughing at one woman's desperation, but with joy for the fact that Max had felt for me the same way I'd felt for him for so long. But now that I had pushed him past the edge, now that I had questioned his loyalty, would he still feel the same way?

"Stephanie, have I ruined everything?"

"I doubt it. Just talk to him. Okay?" She took the wine glass from my hand. "After you sober up."

"How can you be so sure?" I looked into her eyes.

She took my hand in hers and looked directly back into my eyes.

"Samantha, you are one of the most loving and accepting people I know, but you are going to have to take a risk and trust someone eventually. Trust me, I know that Max is dying to hear from you. He is probably wracking his brain right now trying to figure out where the conversation went wrong. This should not be a surprise to you, but Max loves you as much and as deeply as you love him." Stephanie shook her head. "Don't let insecurity rob you of the best time in your life."

I stood up. "You're right! I'm going to go talk to him right now." A wave of dizziness washed over me, a reminder of how much wine I'd guzzled. "Maybe after a nap."

"Definitely after a nap." Stephanie laughed. "I'll leave you to it. Just promise me—no calls, no texting, until your mind is clear."

"Okay, I promise."

After Stephanie left I headed straight to bed. The room spun no matter how still I was. I knew it wasn't just from the wine. It was from my spiraling emotions. One second I felt secure—of course Max loved me—the next, I felt as if I was being foolish to think that he did. By the time I fell asleep, I felt as if an entire war had been fought within my mind.

When I woke up the next morning, I had a headache. I sat up and reached for the stash of aspirin I kept in my bedside drawer. I took a couple, then closed my eyes. I felt as if I had the weight of the world upon me. I owed Max a big apology, but I wasn't sure he would even want to see me.

I was about to curl up for another hour of sleep when I heard a knock at the door. I'd fallen asleep in the clothes I had tossed on the day before. At least I wasn't in my pajamas. I hoped that maybe if I ignored the knock, whoever it was would go away.

I heard another heavy knock.

"Sammy, please let me in."

CHAPTER 11

As soon as I recognized Max's voice I bolted out of bed. I rushed to the door and opened it wide for him.

"Max, I didn't know it was you. I'm so sorry."

"You're not answering any of my calls or texts." He frowned. "Are you still mad about yesterday?"

"You called?" I noticed my phone beside a half-empty glass of wine on the counter. I picked it up. "Oh, Stephanie must have turned it off."

As I was powering the phone back on, Max stepped inside.

"Stephanie?"

"She came over last night."

"Oh, Sammy, please tell me you didn't—"

"No, Max, no. I'm so sorry. I don't know what I was thinking. It wasn't right for me to accuse you."

Max smiled with relief. "I really thought you were still mad."

"Aren't you?" I met his eyes.

"No. I'm not mad at all. I'm just glad that we got all

of this straightened out. Now we can put it behind us."

"I'm glad too. And I'm going to make it up to you." I kissed him.

Max pulled away from the kiss after a moment.

"What do you mean?"

"I mean, I'm really sorry and I'm going to make it up to you."

"I don't want you to make anything up to me. There's nothing to make up. I love you. We had a little spat. It's no big deal, right? It was a misunderstanding."

"But it shouldn't have been. Don't you see? I can't believe I let you think that I didn't trust you. How can you just forgive me for that?"

"Easily. I know you, Sammy. I know trust doesn't come easily for you. That's okay."

"No, it's not." I wrapped my arms around his waist. "It would drive me crazy if I thought you didn't trust me."

"Okay, but I'm not you."

"What does that mean?"

Max laughed. "Exactly that. You think everything has some secret meaning. I don't. If you say you trust me, I believe you."

I couldn't even begin to comprehend being able to be that casual about the idea of trust.

"Don't you think we should work on strengthening that trust between us, though? I mean, for our future?"

"Sammy, what's going on with you? Just a couple

days ago we were fine. You didn't have any of these questions."

"I just think if we value our relationship we should be concerned about it."

"So now I don't value it?" He shook his head. "Sammy, where is this coming from?"

I could tell that he was starting to get frustrated. I knew what I wanted to say to him, but getting the words right, so that he could understand me, was proving to be very difficult.

"Never mind." I shook my head. "I'm sorry I even brought it up."

"Wait, don't be sorry." He kissed my forehead. "I just want you to relax. We love each other, isn't that all that really matters?"

I swallowed back the reasons on the tip of my tongue for why that was not all there was to it. The truth was, Max wasn't the problem. I was the problem. Max, with his easy smile and the love in his eyes, was happy in our relationship. I was the one that needed to work on how I felt.

"Yes." I kissed him. "I love you, Max."

"So, then you'll join me for breakfast?"

"Actually, I have a little bit of a headache."

"I can see why." He nodded toward the wine glass.

My heart sped up. Oh, no. Did Max think I drank too much? Did he think I might be an alcoholic? All at once I could see how wild my mind was going. Why was I so anxious about every little thing?

"Right." I laughed. "I guess Stephanie and I were just making up for lost time."

"Well, she's had it rough. With her ex and all."

"She told you about that?"

"Sure. A little. It's a shame that she had to go through that."

I nodded. I was a little surprised that Stephanie had confided in Max. When had they even had time to talk in depth? Just that quickly, suspicions started creeping back into my mind. I tried to brush away the thoughts.

"She really thought she was in love." I looked into his eyes.

"Sammy, I love you. You know that, don't you?" He brushed his fingertips along my cheek. "I'm always going to love you."

I wanted his words to erase every doubt in my mind. They should have. I had no reason to question him. But I couldn't bring myself to answer him. Instead I leaned up and kissed him with passion. Max wrapped his arms around me and held me firmly in his grasp. He continued the kiss as if he hoped it wouldn't end. I lost myself in the heady pleasure that washed over me. When we finally had to come up for air, Max's cheeks were flushed.

"I guess you do." He laughed a little. "I'll see you later, okay?"

"Dinner?" I did my best to hide the fact that I still hadn't answered him.

"I can't tonight. I have something. Maybe dessert?" He winked at me.

"Don't tease me about dessert, Max, because you know just the way I like it."

"Oh I know." He stole one more kiss. "Hot, dripping, and covered in chocolate sauce."

"Mm, yes, and don't forget the cherry this time."

"I won't, I promise. Mint chocolate chip?"

"Yes, please."

He grinned as he turned to leave.

I watched him go. I expected to feel thrilled; instead I had to wonder what he might have to do that would prevent him from having dinner with me. Did he have a better offer?

"Stop it, Sammy!" I growled at myself. But the more I tried to ignore my worries, the bigger they became.

To distract myself, I called Stephanie. I wanted to see if she could help me straighten out the mess in my head.

"Morning. Do you have a headache too?" Stephanie said, picking up after the second ring.

"I think it's finally gone. I was wondering if you'd like to go to this new bookstore with me. It's just a little shop and I want to see if they'd let me do a reading."

"Oh, that's a great idea. Of course I will. When?"

"After lunch? I need to try to get some work done this morning. I'll text you the address and we can meet there."

"Sounds great. See you then. No wine!"

"No wine!" I laughed.

With the way I'd woken up that morning, I had a feeling it would be a while before I enjoyed any more wine.

CHAPTER 12

Even though I really wanted to make some progress on my book that day, I spent most of my time reading it over. It was strange how some passages felt foreign to me, as if I couldn't have been the one to write them. Others felt as familiar as the tattoo on my wrist. What I was looking for was some insight into why I had so much trouble trusting Max. He had never given me a reason not to trust him. Even the idea of his being Blue and keeping it a secret for so long hadn't really bothered me that much.

What bothered me was the fact that I seemed to have such a hard time believing that he really loved me. Maybe it was because I had seen him with so many beautiful women, women who without question were much more beautiful than me.

I'd been working for so long to build my confidence, but all at once it seemed to have disappeared.

I decided to take some extra time to appreciate my body and how I looked before heading out to meet

Stephanie. I took a long shower, used my favorite lotion, fixed my hair just the way I liked it, and applied my make-up. Then I chose a fun flowing dress to wear. I always felt more confident when I could swish. I swirled the skirt around my legs in front of the mirror. Yes, I had worked hard, and it showed, but still, my reflection didn't come close to mirroring the women that I'd seen Max with.

Before I could dwell on it any longer, I headed out the door.

Stephanie was already at the shop when I arrived. She had her nose poked into a novel I recognized. It was a mystery. Stephanie seemed to have a mind for figuring things out. I hoped she'd be able to help me get to the bottom of things.

"Hi." I stepped up behind her.

"Ah!" She threw the book at me. It hit me square in the chin.

"Ouch!" I grabbed my chin and glared at her.

"Oh my god, I'm so sorry, Samantha." Stephanie tried to apologize but she was laughing too hard. She picked up the book from the floor. "Are you okay?"

"I think so. What's with the literary assault?"

"I'm sorry." She was trying to speak through her laughter. "I started reading this book and I was right at the part where the guy was sneaking up behind her—"

"Oh!" I laughed too. "I remember that part. I slept

with my light on for two nights straight."

"I'm really sorry." Stephanie inspected my chin. "Do you need ice?"

"I'm okay. At least, my chin is."

"Well, you look fantastic." She took a step back. "I love the dress."

"Thanks. I was trying to give myself a little bit of a confidence boost."

"Did it work?"

"I don't know." I shook my head and walked over to a small sitting area. I sat down in an overstuffed chair and tried to think of how to explain myself.

"Samantha, it's not Max again, is it? Please tell me you did not drunk-text him."

"I didn't. I swear. In fact he showed up at my apartment this morning."

"How was he?"

"Not mad at all. He was worried that I was mad."

"See! He adores you. You were worried about nothing."

"Is it nothing, though?" I squeezed my hands together. "It feels like something."

"Even though he's not upset. I don't understand. What does it feel like?"

"Just the fact that I was so quick to doubt him. I feel like he's going to remember that and think that I don't trust him."

"Remember, men sometimes think a little

differently." Stephanie frowned. "I get why you're upset about it, but what can you do?"

"I have to find ways to prove to him that I trust him."

"I don't know. Don't you think that sounds a little strange?" Stephanie shook her head. "I'm sure that Max knows that you trust him."

"How? How could he know?" I sighed. "After accusing him of such an absurd thing I feel like I have a lot to make up to him."

"What about Max? How does he feel about it?"

"He just wants to move on from it. He said it was no big deal. But what if he thinks it's a reason not to propose? I can't let him go on thinking that I don't trust him, when really it was my own insecurities that made me accuse him."

"Alright. Alright, if that's what you think is best, what's your first step?"

"Well, I think it's important that we be in situations where he sees that I trust him."

"Like what?"

"Like tandem skydiving."

"Wow, that's definitely showing trust." Stephanie laughed. "Are there any steps before that?"

"I don't know. Maybe surfing?"

"Oh, that's a great idea! It will get you out in the water and give you and Max a chance to work together."

"And he might be able to save me from a shark." I grinned.

"Okay, well, let's not hope for a shark. Anything else?"

"Well, maybe parasailing?"

"Hm. I'm seeing a theme."

"Yes, a theme where I'm in situations where my life depends on Max. What better way to show him how much I trust him?"

"Okay, I get what you're saying, but I think you're missing the point."

"The point?"

"Trusting Max with your life has never been the problem. Trusting Max with your heart is the issue."

CHAPTER 13

Stephanie's words hit me hard. I realized right away that she was right. I would trust Max to drag me out of alligator-infested waters. I just didn't trust that he could really love me—not as much as I loved him.

"I want to so badly."

"Okay, well, you have time to figure out what's holding you back. I mean, Max is fine with what happened, and he adores you. So just take a breath and realize this isn't a crisis. It's just a tiny roadblock."

"I don't know." I shook my head. "Max is going to realize that this isn't right eventually."

"Samantha." Stephanie pursed her lips thoughtfully, then she took my hand. "I'm only telling you this because we're friends and I would want someone to tell me if it were me."

I nodded, giving her permission to continue.

"I think that you're reading way too much into this. Max loves you and he's always accepted you for who you are."

"Sure he loves me, but obviously he doesn't want to

marry me." I stood up and walked over to the shelf of books that lined the side wall of the shop. "See this? An entire wall of relationship books. An entire wall and I've never read a single one of them! How did I ever think I was going to manage without any of this information?" I picked one of the books from the shelf, skimmed a page quickly, and handed it to Stephanie. "This one says that early signs of mistrust are the leading reason why marriages end in divorce. If one partner acts as if they don't trust the other, then there won't be any stability in the relationship."

"Samantha, this is just a book. It was probably written by some old lady surrounded by cats."

"Oh, that's who I'm going to be, isn't it?" I sank back down in the chair across from Stephanie. "Because when Max doesn't propose, I'll never be able to love again. I'll hole myself up in my apartment and write. I'll need cats to stem my loneliness. Or maybe gerbils. Maybe I'll be an old gerbil lady."

"Wow." Stephanie set the book down on the table between us. "Samantha, I think you need to get out and have some fun."

"No, what I need is for you to see how serious this is, Stephanie. This is my future we're talking about. If I don't nip this in the bud now, Max and I will never travel the world, we'll never have babies, we'll never get matching canes—"

I looked over at Stephanie to see that she was trying

not to laugh. I started to get angry, but then I saw my own reflection in the plastic panel of a book display. I looked wild, with wide eyes, red cheeks, and mussed hair. Maybe Stephanie was right. Had I gotten too carried away?

"What kind of fun?"

"We could go out dancing." Stephanie smiled. "Just you and me."

"Okay, that sounds good." I began to relax. "I haven't danced in a long time. Maybe that's the problem. I've been slacking when it comes to exercise."

"I think a little fun will remind you that things are not as serious as they seem. Sometimes you just have to be patient." She squeezed my hand. "And no more reading these books."

I nodded. "Do you want to go to dinner first?"

"I can't. I can meet you around eight, but there's somewhere I have to be around six. Okay? We can meet up at Evermore. They're having nineties night."

"Okay, that should be fun." I already started to feel more relaxed.

I said goodbye to Stephanie and was about to leave myself when the wall of books caught my attention once more.

How Do You Know He Loves You?

What Can You Do to Avoid Dating Disaster?

Are You Good Enough? Ten Ways to Improve Your Worth.

Each title I read made me feel more insecure. If

relationships were so difficult that this many books had to be written about the topic, it was hard for me to believe that I wouldn't make a mess of things with Max.

I grabbed a few books off the shelf and took them to the counter. The woman who rang me up had a nose ring and bright pink hair. I admired how brave she was with her style choices.

"Anything else for you?" She skimmed her eyes over the titles of the books as she bagged them.

"Anything you would recommend?"

"We have a great new series about gerbils." She smiled brightly.

I was mesmerized by tiny pictures that seemed to be etched onto her teeth. Were there teeth tattoos now? Had I missed that? Was I getting so old that I didn't have a clue what was hip anymore?

"What?"

"Gerbils. You know—the perfect pet." She laughed.

"No, nothing about gerbils, please." I shuddered at the idea.

"If you give them a chance you might like them. Much better company than anything you'll find in these books."

I frowned. This was why I bought most of my books online—judgmental bookstore clerks.

"It's for research. I'm a writer."

"Oh?" She smiled. "Let me guess, romance?"

"Not exactly."

"I get so tired of selling all of these romance novels to people. They act like it's such a great story, but it's not. It's one big lie."

"Well, not for everyone."

"Yes, for everyone. It's not as if love actually works like that. It's not all fluff and passion. There's plenty of darkness in love, and the problem is that the romance novelists gloss over that and make it seem like every relationship is perfect. Then, even though you might be in a perfectly good relationship, just because it doesn't match the romance novel idea of love, you think it's wrong. I mean, how many times can Reginald really toss a woman down with passion without throwing his back out?"

"Huh. I never really thought about that." I laughed a little at the idea of a poor handsome hero from a romance novel tripping and falling from his lady's discarded petticoats. It would really ruin the mood.

"I like love just like the next person—but real love. I mean, I've been with my boyfriend for two years. Sometimes it's great and sometimes it's annoying. Sometimes we fight so loud the neighbors bang on the wall. But that doesn't mean our love isn't real."

"Thanks." I smiled at her.

"You're welcome. But like I said, I highly recommend gerbils."

CHAPTER 14

As I walked out of the bookshop her words soothed my nerves. She was right. I had been ready to throw the idea of love out just because Max and I had one little argument, which wasn't even really an argument. Instead of trying to think about ways it could bring us closer together, I thought of ways that I could transform our relationship back into the romance that I thought it should look like.

Even as friends, Max and I had disagreed on more than one occasion. In fact, that was one reason I trusted Max as much as I did—because he didn't hide how he felt from me, which was exactly what I was doing to him.

I hid how I felt about my disappointment over the lack of a proposal. I hid how I felt about what I imagined between him and Stephanie. All because I didn't think I was worthy of his love. It was the same reason that I'd been so blind for so long that he did love me.

It still seemed impossible to me that he could actually love me.

I had to be honest with myself. My head was a mess.

My emotions were in chaos. Despite the fact that everything should have been fine, I was not fine. I couldn't even figure out exactly why I wasn't fine.

I decided to take a walk along the harbor. There was only one thing that could make the walk along the water more beautiful. That was Max.

I texted him to see if he would join me. Maybe my issues were coming up because I'd been missing out on time with him. He was busy and I was always trying to prioritize my book. Sure, we saw each other every chance we could, but maybe there was too much on our minds.

Be there in ten.

I smiled at the text I received almost instantly after sending the invitation, then I tucked my phone into my back pocket.

I stared out across the water and let the tranquility of it wash over me. I did a few deep yoga breaths and willed my mind to settle into a peaceful state. I was ready to seize the moment and live only in the present.

It was a balmy afternoon, and as usual, the pedestrian traffic along the water was pretty intense. The sea of faces had once made me feel a little lonely; now it just made me feel lucky, because I knew that Max was one of those faces. I was no longer alone in the crowd, and there was only one face that I looked for. Once my great love had been a mystery to me, but now I had the luxury of heading straight for him.

A few boats were making their way into the harbor. Joggers whizzed past me along with a handful of cyclists. I leaned against the railing and took another deep breath. It always amazed me how the tall buildings became hulking monsters in the water's surface. Their reflections were distorted to the point of appearing supernatural, and yet all I had to do to know the truth was look up.

"Hi, beautiful." Max stepped up beside me.

I turned to hug him and nearly knocked over a skateboarder. Luckily he caught himself before he could get hurt.

"Watch it, lady!" He scowled.

"Pedestrian traffic, kid. Nowhere does it say you can use your skateboard!" Max bristled.

I loved it when he stood up for me.

"Shove it, old man!"

Max started to turn as if he might go after the kid, but I grabbed his elbow and steered him back to me.

"Don't go. Stay right here with me." We shared a lingering kiss.

When he pulled away he still looked flustered.

"Old man?" He quirked an eyebrow. "When did we become the old people?"

"We're not old. We're just refined."

"Refined?" He let out a loud laugh. "I don't think we can pass for that."

I wrapped my arms around him. I loved being held by

him. Usually it made me feel as if I was the only person that existed. Tonight it made me feel wonderful, but that pesky concern was still there.

"So what's your thing tonight?"

"Thing?"

"You said you couldn't do dinner because you had a thing."

"Oh, right. Yeah, I do."

"So what is it?" I grinned at him.

"I'm just meeting with someone."

I stared at him. What kind of answer was that? I didn't think it could be more evasive or vague.

Live in the moment, Sammy. Focus on the positive, Sammy. Deep breath in and deep breath out.

"Max why won't you tell me who you're meeting?"

Max's expression tightened. "Sammy, not this again."

"Well, it just seems odd to me."

"It's personal."

Those words actually hurt. What could be so personal that he would need to keep from me? It wasn't like he had to make a visit to the gyno for a check-up. Getting a Pap smear—now that was personal; but meeting with someone shouldn't be. I wanted to ask him a million questions. Then I remembered my conversation with Stephanie. She had warned me that I was reading too much into things.

"Okay." I turned back toward the water.

"Sammy." He slipped his arms around my waist from

behind. "There are some things I have to do alone, you know."

"Like what?"

"Like urinating. I prefer to do that alone. And also eating chicken wings. I really like my privacy when I do that. You know, so I can get as messy as I want."

I laughed and shook my head. "Now you're teasing me. You know that's something I like to do alone."

"Oh, is it? Then I guess we need to do it together some time."

"Sounds good." I leaned my head back against his chest.

In that moment, with the subtle sounds of the harbor around us and his scent drifting over me, I felt foolish. I didn't want to be that girlfriend that gave her boyfriend no freedom. A good attempt at showing Max I trusted him would be to just drop it.

"Don't forget dessert tonight." He smiled and kissed my cheek. "I better get going."

I glanced at my watch. It was getting close to six.

"Alright. Oh, I almost forgot. Stephanie and I made plans to go out dancing."

"That should be fun." There was that easy smile. He didn't question me at all. "If you're too tired for dessert, just let me know."

"I'm never too tired for dessert."

I lingered by the water for a few minutes after he left.

CHAPTER 15

I went back to my apartment to change for dancing. I was sure Stephanie was right. I hadn't been my usual humorous self lately. I needed to do something to brighten my mood.

As I dressed my mind wandered. Who might Max be meeting at six o'clock in the evening? Six. I narrowed my eyes. Stephanie had said she had something at six. Why, why, why did they have to be at the same time? I tried to keep my brain from churning over the possibilities, but the more I tried to resist, the more fixated I became.

I had over an hour before I was supposed to meet with Stephanie. I thought the best thing to do was to keep my mind off the possibility of Max and Stephanie being together. I decided I would head down the street to do some window-shopping. There was one store in particular that I liked to peek into.

As I walked toward the shop, I noticed Max's car parked on the street. It seemed odd to me that he would be so close to my apartment. Then there was also the question of what he could possibly be doing that was personal. My mind spun. Then to make matters worse, I heard a familiar laugh.

"Stephanie?" The name popped out of my mouth. I knew it was Stephanie. I knew her laugh.

Max's car was parked in the street; Stephanie's laugh was coming from one of the shops. I wasn't just being paranoid, they were together!

The reality of the situation hit me so hard that I couldn't even react. A part of me wanted to run right back to my apartment and hide away from it all. Another part wanted to hunt them both down and confront them. My best friend and the love of my life? Why would they do this to me? Not only that, but they had been lying to me about it. Why?

Tears flooded my eyes. I was about to melt down into a shivering mass of horror, when I heard the soothing sound of Max's voice.

"Do you think she'll like it?"

"I know she will."

"Are you sure?"

"I am."

I blinked back my tears and listened more closely.

"It's so hard to make her wait."

"It'll be worth it.

My heart began to beat again. Air filled my lungs. They were talking about me. Max had a romantic night planned for me? Suddenly I understood that Max and Stephanie weren't sneaking around behind my back because of a secret love affair, but because they were working together on a surprise for me. I'd been so fixated on my insecurity that I hadn't even considered that. Even worse, if they caught me listening in, the surprise would be ruined.

I ducked around the side of a building as their voices drew closer.

"So I hear you two are going dancing."

"Don't worry, I'll keep an eye on her." Stephanie laughed.

"Oh, I'm not worried. I know Sammy loves me. She would never do anything to hurt me. I just hope she figures out that I feel the same."

"Just give her time, Max."

"I will."

As their voices faded away I sniffled back the last of my tears. I felt guilty for thinking such horrible things about the two most important people in my life. It was clear that they only had good things planned for me.

If Max was planning a romantic evening, I guessed it might be the proposal that I had been waiting for. I felt soothed by what I'd overheard, but at the same time it bugged me that I had even worried about it in the first place.

I was going out to a dance club and Max wasn't the least bit jealous because he trusted me. I felt bad for not feeling the same way. I wished there was a way to reach deep down inside me and fix whatever was broken.

My phone buzzed to let me know I had a text.

Samantha, where are you? I'm waiting at your apartment.

Be there in a minute, Steph.

I started to step out from behind the building when my phone buzzed again.

Have fun tonight. Looking forward to our dessert.

I smiled at Max's text. Then my heart raced. Could he be planning to propose over ice cream? It would be the perfect time. That would explain why he'd said no to dinner. He probably had to plan the evening. I was giddy with excitement as I hurried back to my apartment. Stephanie was waiting for me outside.

"Where were you?"

"I just went to grab a few things from the corner store."

"Oh?" She looked at my empty hands.

"I forgot my wallet." I grimaced. I wondered if she could tell that I was lying to her. If she could, she didn't call me on it.

"Well, you look fantastic. Are you ready to go dance the night away?"

"Yes, I am!" I smiled.

I couldn't wait to get out on the dance floor and then

get back to my apartment. I had a strong feeling that this was going to be my last night without an engagement ring.

The club was packed. As soon as I walked in, I was reminded of why I didn't go to them very often. The music blasted my ears. The heavy scents of perfume and cologne made me a little sick to my stomach. The flashing lights reminded me that my headache from that morning wasn't completely gone.

"It's great, huh?" Stephanie grinned.

I nodded and managed to smile. I was more determined than ever to have a great time. I wanted to be in a wonderful mood when I met with Max later. I was already rehearsing in my head the way I would accept his proposal.

The dance floor was flooded with handsome men, but I barely noticed them. It was strange that the only face I wanted to see belonged to Max.

"Dance with me."

Somebody grabbed me from behind and whirled me around.

CHAPTER 16

I looked into deep brown eyes that seemed to ooze sensuality. He searched my gaze as he slid his arm around my waist. "Just one dance, bella."

I was prepared to shove him away and decline the offer but it occurred to me that this might be the very last time that I danced with another man. He was devastatingly attractive with a smooth accent to add to the yum factor. Yet I felt no desire for him. It wouldn't have mattered if a model stepped off the front of a magazine, the desire wouldn't be there. It seemed safe to dance with him.

"Alright, one dance."

I did enjoy having that intimate connection with another human being when we danced together. It was a push and pull of bodies, emotions, and trust. As he swirled me around the dance floor, I could hear the sounds of others around me. Some were laughing, some were whispering, some were singing along to the music that played. Everyone was caught up in a ritual of trying to connect with one another.

Out of the corner of my eye I caught sight of Stephanie dancing with a good-looking man. She seemed so happy and relaxed despite her declaration that she had sworn off dating. I knew that I needed to find a way to be that light and free.

I had lightened my body with a healthy diet and exercise. I had lightened my soul with yoga and meditation. But my emotions were still quite heavy. Even though I wanted to focus on the moment, they seemed to drag me right back into the past. The man I was dancing with seemed to notice.

The music died down.

He took my hand. "Did you enjoy it at all?"

"I did. Thank you."

"Then why aren't you smiling?"

"I have a lot on my mind."

"Dancing is supposed to erase all of that." He chuckled. "Maybe you should tell me what's on your mind."

"I'm sorry. I don't mind one dance, but you should know that I'm not interested in anything more than that." I glanced helplessly in Stephanie's direction. She was already dancing with someone else.

"Oh, me either. I just like to dance. But I still don't mind listening." He smiled.

I stared at him for a moment. I shared intimate details of my life on my blog on a regular basis, not to mention the amount of my own feelings that I put into my books.

Would it really be so bad to get a man's perspective on things?

"I don't know. I guess I'm having a difficult time trusting my boyfriend."

"Is he a cheater?"

"No, nothing like that. He's a good man. I just find it hard to believe that he could really be in love with me."

"Oh." He nodded. "I know what your problem is."

"You do?" My eyes widened. Even though I knew it was impossible, I wanted to believe that he would have the answer for me.

"Sure. You've spent too much time alone."

"Huh? We've been together for a year."

"But what about before that?" He tapped his heart lightly. "If the heart isn't used to being open, to being vulnerable, it will fight tooth and nail to stay closed. If you're used to being alone, you're not used to being vulnerable."

"Wow. I never thought of it that way." I hadn't been vulnerable. My heart hadn't been in the hands of someone else.

"It's okay. You just have to be patient with yourself. Some things can't be forced or sped up, you know."

"Thanks." I smiled at him as he walked away.

I was feeling much better than I had before, but I didn't agree with his last words. I wanted to speed it up. With all of my studies and introspective skills, I was sure I could master my issues with vulnerability in time for dessert with Max.

I found Stephanie on the dance floor.

"Do you mind if we go?"

"Sure." She shrugged. She said goodbye to the man she was dancing with. "Is everything okay?"

"Yes. I just want a little time to sort some things out before Max comes over."

"Oh, okay." Stephanie smiled. "I'm glad you're feeling better about that."

I flashed back for a moment to how I felt when I thought Stephanie and Max were playing around behind my back. I'd felt so horrible. But here she was, being the best friend I could have, and supporting me. I knew that I had to keep my anxiety in check.

On the way home Stephanie told me about the men she had danced with.

"I think my biggest problem is that I'm not picky." She laughed.

"Not at all?"

"Not really. As long as a guy has a great smile, I'm willing to give it a shot. I guess I try to see the potential in everyone. Even if it isn't really there."

"That's hard. Because then you have so many to choose from."

"The hard part is not being able to see their flaws. I should have seen them with my ex, but his good qualities seemed more important. That's why I need to take a break from dating. I need to get things clear in my head."

I frowned. I agreed with what she was saying, but I hoped that it didn't hold true for me. Had I rushed into things with Max without getting things clear in my head? I tried not to think too much about it.

CHAPTER 17

I ran back and forth throughout my apartment gathering all the pieces to my plan. I set up candles on the coffee table. I put my favorite playlist on at just the right volume level. I made sure the kitchen was spotless and that wine glasses were conveniently within reach. I checked on the state of my bedroom to ensure that nothing embarrassing could be stumbled upon. I even dumped my bathroom trash. I made sure that the couch cushions were fluffed. Then I changed into my sexiest pajamas.

Okay, they weren't really that sexy. They had a low-cut top, but only because the top was too big on me since losing some weight. The pants were silky and felt nice against my skin. I spent a little time making sure my hair looked mussed, but appealing. Once I was sure that I looked as good as I could for a dessert date, I headed back into the living room to wait.

It was hard to be still. I kept glancing at my phone to check the time and to check for texts. It was getting late. What if he'd forgotten all about our plans? Could I have been wrong about what might be happening tonight? It was obvious to me that Max and Stephanie had had a secret meeting. It had to be about me and it had to be about proposing. This had to be the night.

I closed my eyes and drew a deep breath. I wanted more than anything to be able to control my anxiety and emotions.

I was just about to text Max, to see if he was still coming, when there was a knock on the door. My heart jumped into my throat. This was it. This was the moment that I'd been waiting for. It didn't matter to me any more that there was no photographer to take a picture of the special moment; I just wanted it to happen.

I lunged toward the door and caught my foot on the leg of one of the barstools at the breakfast bar. I tried to catch myself and succeeded in knocking the perfectly placed wine glasses right off the counter.

The crash must have alarmed Max, because he knocked louder.

"Sammy, are you okay?"

I looked at the shattered glass all over the floor. I was not okay. I'd tried to make everything perfect, and now everything was a mess.

"Just a second, Max!"

I grabbed the broom and dustpan. I tried to hurry to clean up the mess but finding the clear glass on the white tile floor was very difficult.

"Sammy, the ice cream is melting."

I sighed and walked over to the door. I was covered in sweat from trying to hurry to clean up the mess. My sexy pajamas stuck to my skin. I opened the door and looked at Max.

"Hi." I frowned.

"Hi." He smiled at me.

"Come in. Just be careful, there's glass on the floor."

"Okay." He nodded and glanced at the mess in the kitchen. "What happened?" He set the white paper bag that held our ice creams down on the breakfast bar.

"Oh, I slipped and knocked over the wine glasses." I picked up the broom and dustpan again.

"Here, let me get it." He took them from me. I protested, but he ignored me.

"Did you have fun with Stephanie?"

"Yes."

He swept the last of the glass into the dustpan. Then he straightened up and looked into my eyes.

"Did you dance with anyone?"

I smiled a little at the question. "Yes."

"Hm." He tossed the glass into the trash and then put the dustpan and broom away. "I'm trying not to be jealous."

"Oh, please, Max, you're not jealous." I rolled my eyes.

"No?" He slid his arms around my waist. I felt his fingertips glide along the silky material that covered my hips. "To think of some strange man with his hands on you…" He pulled me close. "It was driving me crazy."

I kissed his cheek. "You're just trying to make me feel good."

"Nope. If I wanted to do that, I'd do this." He kissed me with such passion that I stumbled back a step. Luckily he held me tight to keep me from falling. When he broke the kiss I laughed.

"Okay, maybe you were a little jealous."

"I trust you, Sammy. That doesn't mean I have to like the idea of some other guy dancing with you, when it should have been me. Sorry I couldn't join you tonight."

"Oh, that's okay. I know you were busy." I bit my tongue to keep from blurting out what I suspected. "Let's get to that ice cream before it melts."

"Good idea."

He carried the bag over to the living room.

"Oh, candles." He winked. "Nice."

"Thanks. I just thought tonight might be special."

"Any night with you is special." He sat down beside me and opened up the bag. He handed me my ice cream. I took the lid off carefully.

"You remembered the cherry. Thank you."

"Of course. And I like the music." He swayed a little. "Maybe we'll get to dance after all."

"Maybe." I smiled.

I used the long plastic spoon that came with the ice cream to poke around through the chocolate sauce. I was sure that the ring had to be hidden somewhere inside.

The more I moved the ice cream around, the more sure I became.

"Is there something wrong with it?" Max looked at me with a raised eyebrow.

"No, it's fine."

"Then why aren't you eating it?"

"Oh, right." I laughed and took a careful bite. I swirled the ice cream around to be sure there was nothing hidden in it before swallowing. "Yum."

"Sammy, I wanted to talk to you about the other day. I mean, I know I said it was fine but—"

I braced myself. I knew that it would get to him eventually. He would see that I hadn't trusted him and that it was a problem.

"I know, Max, I know."

'You do?" He looked at me with surprise.

"I mean I know why you're upset."

"You're the one that should be upset." He shook his head. "I never should have walked out. I should have stayed and we could have talked it through. It's just, if I feel myself getting angry, I try to avoid it. I don't like to get worked up."

CHAPTER 18

I stared at Max in disbelief. I couldn't believe that he was apologizing to me.

"Max, you did the right thing."

"Did I?" He shook his head and took a bite of his ice cream. "When we're married, I don't want you to ever feel like I'm walking out on you."

My heart fluttered at the mention of the "m" word. Was he telling me this to iron things out before I found the ring? I was so excited that I almost forgot to respond.

"Max, I love you. I shouldn't have been so upset."

"Hey, things are going to happen in our lives that makes us angry, or jealous, or upset. We have to be ready to handle that, right? Walking away is not handling it."

"Maybe, but it gives us both a chance to cool off." I scraped the bottom of the container.

So far I'd not found a ring. My heart sank when I realized there wasn't one hidden there. Maybe he had it in his pocket instead? Maybe he worried that the ice cream would ruin the stone?

"Sammy, I just want you to know how important you

are to me. No matter what happens in our lives, we should be there for each other—just like we always have been. I don't want anything to change that."

"Nothing will." I took his hand in mine and looked into his eyes. "Nothing can."

"Are you sure? Because I think if we let things go as they were going the other morning, it could have gotten very difficult."

I frowned. "You're right. I'm sorry. I was being unreasonable."

"I don't know that you were. All I know is that I want to be confident that our relationship is strong—that we can overcome anything we need to."

"Max." I squeezed his hand. When he met my eyes it dawned on me. It was something that had never occurred to me before. Max was scared. "Are you afraid?"

"I'd be lying if I said no." He frowned. "Before I realized that I was in love with you, I thought I had my life figured out. I thought I knew everything about how my life should go. But you know, going forward—starting our lives together—that's a big change."

I wrapped an arm around his shoulder and hugged him. "Oh, Max, it's not that much of a change if you think about it. We've been part of each other's lives for so long. That part is never going to change."

"You know I love you, don't you, Sammy?" He kissed my forehead. "Nothing will ever change that."

I nodded. Still, I felt a pang in my heart. Did I really

know that? There was obviously no ring in the ice cream. Now Max was talking as if he was getting cold feet. So how could I know that?

"I love you too, Max."

"I know you do." He smiled. He leaned close for a kiss.

It was a sweet kiss with traces of ice cream left on our lips. It should have been a perfect moment. Instead it was tainted by my concern. I was lying to Max, and he was worried about the future. He had every reason to worry, since I could not bring myself to be honest with him.

"I guess I should get going."

The last thread of hope in my heart that he might surprise me with a proposal snapped. There was no special night planned. Whatever he had been talking to Stephanie about didn't pertain to our dessert.

"I guess."

I sat back and stared at the empty styrofoam cup on the table.

"Why does it feel like you're not telling me something?" There was clear frustration in Max's voice.

My stomach twisted with conflict. I knew that Max wanted me to tell him how I was feeling, and in the past when we were best friends, I never would have hesitated to. Now I felt like if I told him the truth he would see the crazy I was trying to hide from him and want nothing to do with me. How could I tell him that I didn't understand why he hadn't proposed?

"I just overheard something tonight that I probably shouldn't have."

"What do you mean?"

"I mean why were you and Stephanie together tonight, when neither of you told me you would be?"

I might have imagined it, but it seemed to me Max's skin grew pale.

"Oh, you saw us?"

"I heard you."

"Why didn't you say something?"

"I don't know."

"We just ran into each other. I stopped in to pick something up and Stephanie happened to be there."

I frowned. I could see that happening. Stephanie was on her way to meet me, so she had stopped at the shop. Why Max was there? That, I didn't know.

"It just seems odd to me that the two of you would run into each other that way."

"You think we planned it?"

"I don't know what to think."

"Sammy, there's nothing between Stephanie and me. You know that, don't you?"

I nodded.

"Are you sure?" He cupped my cheeks with his hands. "I would never do anything to hurt you."

"I'm okay. I promise." I kissed him again. Then I walked him toward the door. "Hey, I was thinking about learning to surf. Is that something you'd like to do with me?"

"Sure, I guess." He scratched his head. "It could be fun."

"Great." I smiled. "I'll let you know when I set up the lessons."

He looked into my eyes one last time. "I love you, Sammy."

"I love you too, Max. Thanks for the dessert."

CHAPTER 19

That night I found it very difficult to sleep. All I could think of was the bottom of that container. I'd worked myself up yet again. I believed that Max was going to propose. Why else had he and Stephanie been whispering and sneaking around? I thought I'd put my suspicions about them to rest, but now I wasn't so sure. What if Max and Stephanie were talking about me because they were worried about me? The more I went over in my head the reasons why Max might not want to marry me, the worse I felt.

He had a stable career with a good income. I was a writer. Sure, I was doing pretty well for myself, but that didn't change the fact that it wasn't exactly a stable career. Maybe Max was waiting for me to grow up a little? It hurt my heart to think that he didn't believe in my writing. Then I realized that I was inventing Max's feelings. I had no idea how he really felt abut my writing. He had never been anything but supportive about it.

So why no ring?

I turned over and punched my pillow. I hated feeling

so anxious. I was worried that I didn't trust Max, and I was worried that the proposal I'd expected was never going to happen. Maybe that was the problem. Max had never told me that he would propose by a certain time. So why was I stuck on the idea that he was going to now? I was waiting and waiting only to be disappointed. But whose fault was that?

I sighed and buried my face into the pillow. I decided I would turn over a new leaf in the morning. I didn't want Max to think I was clingy or demanding. I'd let my emotions and worry distract me from making any real progress on my book.

I would wake up and refuse to think about marriage or the future. In fact, I would spend as little time as possible with him. I would focus on my writing and on getting my diet and exercise plan back on track. I had a future, even if Max wasn't sure if he wanted to be in it. I still had to prepare for it.

When I woke up the next morning I felt the weight of my thoughts the night before. It was hard to believe that I'd let myself spiral so fast. I'd gone from being self-aware and self-confident to drowning in my insecurities.

I sent Max a text.

I'm going to be working as much as possible. Love you.

Then I turned my phone off. I was not going to let anything distract me.

I spent the next half hour going through withdrawal. I was used to having constant contact with Max. If I wondered about him and his day, I could just text him. If I wanted to go out for lunch, I could give him a call to see if he wanted to join me. But with my phone off, I felt very disconnected.

Still, I resisted turning it on.

I focused on the book I was working on. I couldn't expect to be an inspiration to women if I was sitting around waiting for a man to propose to me. The very thought made my stomach churn. I had really gotten off my path of healthy self-esteem.

As I began to type, all of the things I'd learned over the past year came back to me. I had to remain in my peace, I had to stay focused in the present. If that meant limiting my time with Max until I could get over the hurt of the proposal that never happened, then that was what I would have to do.

I felt uneasy as I wrote about relationships in the book. I was beginning to wonder if relationships were ever something I could master. I remembered what the man at the club had said to me. I had gotten too used to being alone. Would I ever be able to open my heart?

I tried to distract myself by eating at home and not leaving my apartment. I didn't want to be tempted to call Max.

It was nearly evening when I got an e-mail. I was a little startled, as it was from the address that Max had used when he pretended to be Blue.

Hello? Are you okay? I've been trying to reach you all day.

It was nice that he'd noticed that I was missing, but I wasn't sure that I wanted to give in and turn my phone on just yet.

Sorry, been busy with work. Writing is my career, you know.

I didn't really think about how annoyed that sounded until after I sent the e-mail. Max responded a few seconds later.

Yes, I know. I'm sorry for interrupting. Let me know when you come up for air. Love you.

My fingers hovered over the keyboard as I thought about what I wanted to send back to him. There were a million things that I wanted to say, but I knew that they would start a conversation, I knew I would get pulled back into my insecurities. I just needed a breather from the chaos that was my love for Max.

Love you too.

I sent the e-mail knowing that Max would be a little put off by how short and vague it was. But for once I didn't obsess about it.

It struck me that I needed to find Samantha—not Sammy, who was in love with Max—but Samantha, the woman, the writer, the bucket list Olympian.

I needed to feel one hundred percent whole again.

CHAPTER 20

Instead of just tuning back into my writing, I decided to tune back into my go-to inspirational websites. There were a few blogs that I'd been following the past year for the uplifting messages I found there. Of course I had a large collection of inspiring memes too. I needed to be reminded of how far I'd come along my journey.

I felt the strange sensation of getting lighter. Even though I knew realistically that I hadn't lost any weight, I felt as if a weight had been lifted off me.

By the end of the day, I felt more secure than ever. I turned my phone back on. I found that I had a dozen texts from Stephanie. I had half that amount from Max. I was tempted to call him, but decided to connect with Stephanie first.

I dialed her number.

"Oh, so you are alive?" She laughed when she picked up the phone.

"Last time I checked." I laughed too.

"What's going on?"

"I was working. Just wanted to catch up on some

things. What's going on with you?"

"You mean other than going through Samantha withdrawal?"

"Ha ha."

"I mean it. You can't just not text me. It's not cool." She laughed again.

"I'm sorry. To be honest, I'm having a hard time keeping my head clear."

"Why?"

"Ah well, you know."

"Max?"

"Max."

"Samantha, I don't understand what you're worried about. He clearly adores you."

I cringed. I didn't even know how to explain it myself. "I guess I'm just feeling a little strange about why things aren't moving forward."

"You have to stop worrying so much. Just let things happen as they will. Trust me."

"Thanks."

While I was on the phone with Stephanie, it vibrated to let me know that I had a text.

"Stephanie, I've got to go."

"Okay, but don't be a stranger. I've really enjoyed us hanging out so much lately."

"I know. Me too."

When I hung up the phone I looked at the text.

Are you still going to meet me for the surfing lesson?

I frowned. I'd forgotten about setting up the class earlier. I didn't exactly feel strong enough to meet up with him, but at the same time I couldn't avoid him much longer. If the shoe was on the other foot and it was Max not contacting me, I would be losing my mind.

Yes. I'll be there. Love you.

It was a short text, but I hoped it reassured him.

So you're coming up for air?

I smiled at the text.

For a little while.

I waited a moment, as I expected him to text back. When I didn't receive any more texts I put the phone down.

The surf lesson was in the morning, and that meant I was going to have to get into a swimsuit. It had been a while since I put one on. I dug around in my drawer and found the one I had most recently purchased. It fit okay in the store, but looking at it made me anxious as I wondered if it would still look okay. Over the past few weeks I hadn't done a great job of following my diet and exercise routine.

I changed into the suit and then turned to look in the mirror. All I could see was flaws. My thighs were flabby. My arms drooped. My breasts sagged. I didn't even want to think about the mound of fat around my waist. I was very disappointed. The suit fit the same as it had in the store, but clearly I'd lost sight of my beauty. A flicker of panic rushed through me. I couldn't let Max see me like this. He would go running for the hills. I was sure of it. My chest ached with anxiety.

I was about to grab my phone to cancel the lesson, when I realized how that would seem to Max. It would hurt him if I cancelled our plans. As I thought about it more, I realized this was an opportunity to trust Max. Max had never been anything but kind about the way I looked. I had no real reason to think he would be any different the next morning. It was just my panic and insecurity talking.

I took a deep breath and forced myself to look in the mirror again. Okay, I might have put on a pound or two, but not much. I hadn't been exercising as much, so I wasn't as toned, but the suit still fit.

"Sammy, you've got to get a grip." I shook my head at myself. "Max loves you."

Even saying that out loud in my empty bedroom to my worried reflection felt like a risk. Was I ever going to believe it?

I changed back into my suit and decided that I needed

more than inspiring websites and memes, I needed some face-to-face inspiration. I put a call in to the meditation teacher that I'd been working with. There were no classes that night, but he said he would meet me with me for a private session.

I felt relieved. I needed some serious inner-self time.

As I left the apartment I grabbed my phone. I noticed that Max still hadn't texted me back. I was tempted to text him to see what he was up to, but I knew I had no right. I was the one that was being distant, not him. I just hoped that he would understand while I worked to get myself together again.

CHAPTER 21

I'd never attended a private session with my meditation teacher before. I was looking forward to having the one-on-one focus.

When I knocked lightly on the door of the classroom I heard music playing inside. I was pulled in by the peaceful sound of it. I opened the door to find my meditation teacher cross-legged and peaceful—that much I expected. What I did not expect was that he wouldn't be wearing any clothes.

"Oops, I'm so sorry. I must be early." I backed out of the room.

"It's okay, Samantha. Here." He spread a towel across his lap. "Does that make you feel more comfortable?"

I was going to point out that he still didn't have clothes on, but I decided against it. Why should I feel uncomfortable around him in his natural state? He obviously fully accepted his body and expected me to as well. I had no concerns about his intentions.

"Okay, thanks." I stepped back into the room. "Are you sure I'm not intruding?"

"Not at all." He gestured to the cushion in front of him. "Get comfortable and settle in. We'll do a quick guided meditation."

I sat down in front of him. I thought about taking my clothes off, but decided against it. He said to get comfortable, not get naked.

As soon as I was settled he began speaking. I closed my eyes and let his voice take me on a journey. It didn't matter what he looked like, or what his name was; the lilt of his voice was the most relaxing thing I'd ever experienced.

My body began to relax. My mind, however, was a different story. I found it very difficult to let go of my racing thoughts. In my head, I was warring over whether I could accept Max's love or not. I wanted to trust him, to believe that he loved me, but there were so many reasons why he wouldn't.

I sighed and tried to focus past those thoughts. I needed to find my place of peace, where I could hear that still voice.

Deeper and deeper I drifted into my own thoughts. Flashes of being teased as a child, moments of embarrassment as an adult, all flooded my mind. It was as if my psyche was attempting to break down any chance of my building confidence. Worst of all was the way I felt about my writing. On the surface, I was confident and proud of what I'd created, but underneath I wondered if I would ever be a great writer. Anyone could type out a few words and string them together into a book. It took a true writer to create a great story.

Deeper and deeper I drifted, hoping that I could reach some part of myself that was confident.

As I fought my way toward this peaceful place, I didn't really notice the sound that surrounded me. It wasn't until I felt a rush of water against my skin that I opened my eyes. I was confused at first. I wondered if I'd been dreaming. I forgot where I was and why I was there. Water hitting my skin made no sense to me.

"Samantha, Samantha, we have to leave the room."

My teacher stood over me, clinging to his towel. I noticed that his skin was dripping wet too. I looked up to see that the sprinklers in the ceiling were spraying water everywhere.

"I'm sorry. I must have knocked over one of my candles and slipped into a trance. The fire department is on its way. There's no danger, but we have to leave the room so that they can evaluate the situation."

I pulled myself to my feet. I was relieved that I'd left my clothes on.

"Don't you have something to put on?"

"That's what caught on fire." He smiled sheepishly. "I guess the lesson today is to accept my vulnerability."

That word struck me as we hurried out of the room. It was the second time someone had mentioned it to me. As I stood beside him and watched the firefighters march inside, I felt grateful not to be the one wearing a towel.

Then I glanced down at my shirt. My white *thin* shirt. I could clearly see my bra—and more—through it.

I ducked behind the man who was covering himself with only a towel. Somehow I felt more exposed than he was.

Maybe that was the problem.

I had been through circumstances where I'd been exposed physically due to an accident or other issues, but I'd never willingly exposed myself. Even with Max, we were taking things very slow physically. But it wasn't just about my physical body. It was also about my heart. I hadn't exposed that either.

I decided in that moment that I was going to try to be more vulnerable.

Making the choice to be more vulnerable opened up an entire new world to me.

Lately, I'd been using all of my energy to prevent myself from being vulnerable. I did what I could to keep from ever leaving myself open to being hurt.

Now I knew that if I wanted to find a way to trust Max, I was going to have to take a risk and expose myself in ways I never considered possible.

My fingers flew across the keys, not limited by my insecurities attempting to tuck myself safely away from the words I was writing.

By the time I curled up in bed I'd gotten more work

done in a few hours than I had all week. I even fell asleep without having to convince my mind to slow down.

CHAPTER 22

Before I knew it the alarm clock beside my bed was buzzing. I was reluctant to wake up. Since becoming a writer, I'd let myself sleep and wake when I pleased. An alarm had become a relic of my life as a working stiff. But I'd set it to make sure that I woke up in time for my surfing lesson with Max.

I pulled myself out of bed and half-stumbled into the bathroom after putting my bathing suit on.

All that I'd discovered about vulnerability went right out the window when I looked at myself in the mirror. The thought of Max seeing me in my bathing suit made me cringe. I grabbed a large white nightgown that I'd kept from my larger days. I pulled it on and was satisfied to see that it covered every inch of me. Maybe being exposed was supposed to help me learn to trust, but I wasn't ready for that exposure to take place in a bathing suit.

I heard a sharp knock on the door and knew that it was Max. I rushed to let him in.

Seeing Max standing there was like taking a breath for the first time.

"What are you wearing?" Max did his best to smile but his eyebrow was still raised.

"It's just a cover-up. So I don't get cold on the way."

"I see." He tilted his head to the side. "I don't think you're in any danger of freezing." He held his hand out to me. "It's good to see you. I missed you."

My heart melted at his words. I hugged him and breathed in the scent of his cologne. It hit me then that I had missed him too. I might have been trying to find myself, but Max was a part of all parts of me. I held him so tight that he must have noticed.

"As much as I'm enjoying this, we're going to miss our lesson if we don't get going. It seemed important to you when you suggested it."

"You're right." I took one more deep breath of his scent and then pulled away from him.

"You okay, sweetheart?"

"I am."

"You would tell me if you weren't?"

"Sure."

He shook his head but he didn't question me any further. He held the door open for me.

Max's car was always one of my favorite places to be. I had yet to figure out why. Maybe it was that his radio always seemed to be playing a good song. Or maybe it was because he'd kept the same brand of vanilla air freshener in it since we were in college. I always associated it with a fun place to be. That morning was no different.

"I'm really glad you planned this. We haven't been out on many adventures together lately."

I smiled. "I love getting to spend time with you."

"Do you?" He stared through the windshield.

"What do you mean? Of course I do."

"I mean, if you think I'm holding you back from success, all you have to do is tell me."

"Oh, Max, I don't think that at all. I just needed to refocus."

"On something other than me." He laughed a little. "I can see why you would need to do that." He turned in to the parking lot beside the beach.

"It's not like that at all, Max, I promise."

He frowned and turned off the car. Then he looked over at me. "Sammy, I get that we're separate people, we're going to have separate emotions, and that sometimes you're going to need some space. I just want to know what's going on in your head, that's all. Okay?"

"Okay." I nodded. I almost told him the truth, but I still couldn't bring myself to do it.

We walked down toward the water. The morning air was warm already. Max headed straight for the edge of the water.

"Are you going to take that off?" He sunk his feet into the shallow water.

"I don't know. It's pretty sunny. Maybe I should just leave it on." I kicked my feet through the sand.

"Sammy." Max's hands seized my hips. "The only reason I got up this early with a smile on my face was because I knew I would get the chance to see you in a swimsuit."

"Oh, please." I rolled my eyes.

He tightened his grip on my hips. "What?"

"Oh, Max, you don't have to pretend that you find my body appealing in a swimsuit." I shook my head.

"Samantha!" He sighed and tugged me close to him. "Is that what this cover-up is all about? Do you think I don't adore every inch of you? I mean, seriously, Sammy, what have we been doing for a year if you really don't think I find you attractive?"

"I just feel uncomfortable in only a swimsuit."

"You should never feel uncomfortable around me, Sammy. I adore you. You're gorgeous."

"I'd be gorgeous if I was a size two." I started to turn away from him.

He turned me back toward him by pivoting my hips.

"That's true, you would be. You would also be gorgeous at a size twenty-eight—just like you're gorgeous now." He sighed with frustration. "I don't understand why that's so hard for you to believe."

"You forget, Max. I've seen the women that you've dated. None of them were my size—not even Stephanie."

"You're bringing up Stephanie now?" Max's eyes

narrowed. "Fine, you saw the women I dated. I saw the men you dated. None of them looked just like me. So what? Were you not attracted to any of them?"

I frowned. He had a point. It always aggravated me when he had a point. "It's not the same and you know it."

"Why? Because you've decided that I can't possibly be attracted to you? Is that what you really believe, Sammy?" He lifted his hands from my hips to my waist and, as if he could see the hesitation in my eyes, he shook his head. "No, I want a real answer this time. Is that what's been going on with you? You think I'm not attracted to you? Because we both agreed to take things slow, and I've tried to be respectful of that."

"I know. No, it's not what I believe."

"Then prove it."

"How?"

"Take it off. Right now. I want to see your beautiful body. That's why I skipped my coffee this morning."

CHAPTER 23

I laughed, but Max's expression was stern. I could tell
that he wanted me to do what he asked. I just wasn't sure
if I could bring myself to do it. There were joggers on the
beach. Not to mention the surf instructor, who was
heading toward us. He looked like he had never eaten a
carb in his life, or met a weight he couldn't lift. Yet Max
wanted me to pull the cover-up off in front of him and all
these other people?

"Maybe we should just go. This was a bad idea."

"No. Sammy, you just told me that you believed I was
attracted to you. Don't you know how proud I am to be
with you? Don't you think I want to show you off now
and then? I mean, I know that's a chauvinistic thing to
say, but it's the truth. Don't you believe that?"

I lowered my eyes. I absolutely did not believe it.
Most of the time I figured that Max just loved my
personality so much that he could overlook my body. The
idea of his wanting to show me off never even crossed
my mind.

"Please, Sammy. After all the hard work you've done,

you should be so proud of yourself. I loved you a bucket list ago, I love you just as much now. But I feel like you're hiding yourself from me."

I looked out at the swimmers in the water, then back at Max. To him, it was a simple thing that he was asking from me, but for me, it was akin to moving a mountain. He was right, though. I had worked very hard on building my confidence. A few months before, I would have already been playing in the water with him. But since he hadn't proposed, all of my insecurities had come back up.

"I'm not hiding." I looked into his eyes. "I love you, Max."

"Then take this off." He grabbed the hem of the cover-up, but he didn't lift it. Instead, he took my hand and guided it to the hem. "I'm not going to watch you hide yourself when you should be proud of your beauty. Plus, I was looking forward to putting sunscreen on your back."

I had to laugh a little at his crooked smile. Max always knew how to break the tension for me and put me at ease. I took a deep breath of the sea air. I remembered that in order to trust, I was going to have to be vulnerable.

I tugged the hem of the cover-up up along my body and started to tug it off. At least I tried to. I couldn't quite get it past my shoulders, and had somehow gotten my elbows wedged in. As I wiggled in an attempt to free myself I heard Max trying not to laugh. Then I felt his hands freeing me from my cover-up cocoon. When he finally got it off, he tossed it into the sand.

"Beautiful." He smiled at me. I noticed that he took the time to appreciate every aspect of my figure. I'd have thought I would be mortified by his looking so intently at me. Instead, I felt like a work of art. He looked at me with such love in his eyes, that I remembered it was possible to love my body exactly the way it was.

"You two ready to head out?"

The surf instructor had walked up, and I hadn't even noticed him. The joggers still jogged. The swimmers still swam. But I didn't care. Max looked at me with so much affection that I wondered if he might try to cancel the lesson after all.

"We're ready." Max took my hand in his. "We just need a minute to apply sunscreen."

The instant Max started rubbing sunscreen on to my back, all of my regret about taking my cover-up off vanished. He massaged my shoulders a little when he was finished.

"I think I did a good job."

"My turn?" I grabbed the tube from him.

"Oh yeah, slather it on. I've been stuck in the office way too long. I don't want to get crispy."

I savored the opportunity to apply sunscreen to Max. He had a bunch of little freckles along his shoulder blades. I'd seen him shirtless plenty of times. He always kept himself fit, but I didn't care about that. My favorite part of his body were those little freckles. I lost myself in the sweeping motion as I coated his back.

"Guys, we only have an hour!"

The instructor's voice jolted me out of the relaxed state I'd settled into.

"Don't stop." Max glanced over his shoulder at me.

"Max, we have the class."

"Ah, fine." He sighed.

I kissed his cheek. I didn't even care that he tasted like sunscreen. I was certain that our day together was going to be magical.

The instructor took some time with us to teach us about the board. On the sand he showed us how we should climb on the board and how to stand up.

"You guys have this. Why don't you take one out on the water and you can take turns practicing?"

I was looking forward to getting in the water. I was already covered in sand and, although my swimsuit still fit well, it was starting to chaff in unexpected places.

Max picked up one of the boards and waded into the water. I followed close behind him.

"Go right past the breakers, no further. I will have my eye on you."

"I don't know about this." Max laughed. "I don't think I'm going to be able to get up on this thing."

"Sure you will." I steadied the board. "I'm here to help."

"Great."

CHAPTER 24

Max hopped up onto the surfboard. It was slippery and he slid right off the other side.

"Max, are you okay?" I tried not to laugh.

He came sputtering to the surface. "I think so. Oh, you think it's funny?"

"No!" I giggled.

"Okay, your turn." He held the board as I tried to climb on. With all of the sunscreen I'd applied, I was quite slippery. I slipped and slid all over the board but managed to hold on. I tried to get to my feet.

"You're doing it! You're doing it!" Max grinned.

I was doing it. I really was. Until a wave broke over the board and washed me right off it. I flipped under the water and couldn't tell if I was upright or upside down. I felt around for the board—for anything to pull me up out of the water. Max grabbed me by the arm and pulled me up.

"Are you okay?"

I gasped for air. My eyes burned from the salt water. It had been terrifying to feel like I would never find the surface. I clung to Max tightly. He held me in his arms and I felt how fast his heart was pounding. I knew then that he had been as frightened as I was.

"Maybe no more surfing?"

"No more surfing." I nodded against his chest.

He plucked the surfboard out of the water and tucked it under his arm. He kept his other arm around me as we made our way to the shore. The instructor, who had promised to have his eye on me, was busy flirting with a jogger.

"Are you guys done?"

"Yes." Max and I answered at the same time.

"That was quite an adventure." Max led me to the car. He pulled out a couple of towels from the trunk and handed me one.

As I dried off I thought about putting my cover-up back on, but I decided against it. I felt comfortable around Max again. He had proven yet again that I could trust him with my life—but I still wasn't sure about my heart.

"You doing okay? That was pretty scary." He rubbed the towel along my arms to warm me up.

"I'm okay. Good thing you were there."

"I will always be here." He hugged me. "I love you."

I willed myself to believe him. I wanted to feel that trust for him in the core of me. All I could think was—*Until you get bored, until you get tired of me, until you find someone pretty and younger.*

"Sammy?" He rested his forehead against mine. "You're not going to break my heart, are you?"

The question startled me right out of the parade of insults in my mind. Did Max really think I was capable of breaking *his* heart? Did he really think I would ever want anyone other than him?

"Max, why would you ask me that?"

He frowned and pulled away so that he could look into my eyes. "I know that you've watched me go through relationships like I was changing clothes. I know that in the past I acted like I would never fall in love. To be honest with you, I've never been this vulnerable before. I cared about the women I was with, but I wasn't in love with them. I'm in love with you. I also know you. I don't know why, but I know that you're holding back. I'm just telling you now, if this isn't what you want, be honest with me. Let me know now. Okay?"

My heart lurched with every word he spoke. Had I been so caught up in my own insecurities that I was completely blind to the fact that Max had plenty of his own? I was horrified that he would even question my love for him. That was when the sick feeling hit the pit of my stomach as I realized that I was doing the same to him.

"I'm not going to break your heart, Max. I promise."

"I believe you." He smiled just enough to put me at ease. Then he took both of my hands in his. "I'm not going to break your heart either. Do you believe me, Sammy?"

I parted my lips to answer, but he shook his head.

"Don't. The answer doesn't matter to me as much as it does to you. I want you to know the answer."

"Max, it's been an amazing year."

"First of many, right?"

"Right." I kissed him.

As we drove back toward the apartment Max glanced over at me. "Do you want to check out that new movie you wanted to see? I'm free all day."

"No, I can't. I've got to get some work done."

"But you've been working." He stared out through the windshield. "I thought maybe we'd have some time to spend together today."

"I'm sorry, Max—it's just that I got stuck on this one chapter and I can't seem to move forward from it. I really need to just dig into it and see if I can make some real progress."

"Okay. You know I support your writing, but is there going to be some time for us to get together soon?"

"Sure, of course there will be. You're busy, I'm busy." I shrugged.

He looked over at me. Then he turned into the parking lot of my apartment building. I thought he had dropped the subject. Until he parked the car and looked over at me again.

"I'm not too busy to make time for you, Sammy. I'm telling you, I'd like to see you. Some time soon. Okay?"

"Okay." I nodded. I wanted to tell him to come in

and spend the day with me—that we should go to the movies, or just hang out. But I didn't. Because the question he asked me was still rolling around in my head. I was afraid that he was going to ask me again.

"So you'll text me?"

"Yes."

"Promise?"

"Yes." I leaned over and hugged him. "Soon."

CHAPTER 25

As I walked into my apartment I felt a wave of guilt wash over me. More than anything, I wanted to be able to answer Max's question.

I took a shower to wash off the sand. I remembered what it felt like to have him pull me up out of the water. I loved him so very much, and I felt like I was putting everything that we had together at risk, all because I couldn't get over this last hurdle of trust.

I dressed for the day and decided to at least attempt to work. I wasn't really behind—and I felt rather terrible for telling Max that—but I needed to feel like I was getting somewhere. I hoped that if I immersed myself in my book, I'd find some secret as to why I couldn't move forward.

As soon as I started typing, I felt my world shift. It was much easier to slip into the world of fiction that I created than it was to deal with the reality of the chaos that my life had become.

After lunch and a few more chapters, I was very sore

from sitting at the computer for so long. I also felt disconnected and strange as I tried to re-enter the real world. I decided a good dose of yoga would help with the stiff body as well as the stuck mind.

I popped in one of my DVDs and turned on my favorite song on my phone. I popped in my earbuds and began stretching into the positions that the limber woman on the television screen made look so easy. They were not easy for me, though with practice they'd gotten a bit easier.

As I stretched, I closed my eyes. I knew the routine by heart. I used the DVD for timing and to correct my movements when they felt off-kilter. My muscles began to warm almost as soon as I started. It wasn't long before I felt downright hot. I tugged off my top so that I was just in my bra. Then I continued to stretch. I was getting so into the flow of the music and the movement that I didn't notice when my apartment door opened. It wasn't until the DVD ended that I pulled out my earbuds.

"Sammy."

"Oh my god!" I jumped up from the mat and got my feet caught in my discarded shirt. My arms swung like bicycle spokes as I tried to catch myself.

Max rushed forward and caught me easily, sweat-soaked shirt-free skin and all.

"I'm sorry. I didn't mean to scare you." He winced. "I knocked, you didn't answer. I let myself in and I didn't want to interrupt you."

"You were watching me?" I looked into his eyes as I straightened up.

"I couldn't help it. You were mesmerizing."

"It's okay, Max. I just didn't expect to see you."

"Look, I know that we talked about this earlier, but I just didn't feel right about it. Sammy, am I going crazy?" He stared into my eyes. "Is this all in my head or are you really pulling away from me?"

Confronted by the fear in his eyes, my heart ached with regret. I had let Max get to the point of doubting my love for him.

"No, you're not crazy." I blinked back tears.

"Sammy." Max swept his hand back through his hair as if he needed to see more clearly. "Are you saying that you don't want to be with me?"

"No, that's not what I'm saying—not at all!" I grabbed his hands and pulled him toward me. It was such a reckless motion that it nearly knocked us both off balance. "I love you, Max. I'm just having a hard time accepting that you really love me."

"But why?" Max drew his hands away from mine and shook them with frustration. "I've gone out of my way to make sure that you know how I feel about you. You are the love of my life. Why do you continue to doubt that? Is it something I'm doing? Is it something that I'm not doing?"

"No, Max, it has nothing to do with you. I just can't seem to get my head on straight."

"Sammy, you used to tell me everything. Now I feel like everything is a secret, or a vague response, or at best a short little text."

"Max, I—"

"Listen, I'm not trying to force you into anything that you don't want."

"I do want it!"

"Then why are you doing this?" He shook his head. "I feel like one minute we're back to normal and the next you're just gone."

"I had my feelings hurt." I didn't know what else to say it, how else to explain it.

"I hurt your feelings? How?"

"No, I hurt my own feelings. Max, it's impossible for you to understand." He stared at me with heat in his eyes.

"You're right, it is. Because you won't tell me. I need some air." He turned and walked out of the apartment.

I started to go after him but when the outside air hit my chest I remembered that I was shirtless. I shivered a little and ducked back inside to grab my shirt. Before I could, Max stepped back inside.

"I'm sorry. I shouldn't have come over."

I tugged my shirt on. "That's not true, Max. I love seeing you."

"But you have something going on. That should be enough, I guess. You shouldn't have to explain yourself to me."

"I promise. I'm trying to figure it all out."

He nodded, then met my eyes. "I know you are. Just let me know if there's anything I can do to help."

He offered a light kiss. I noticed it was a little quick and cold. I couldn't blame him. Max was confused. I was too. I wanted to be happy, I wanted to trust him, but somehow I couldn't get my heart and my brain to connect.

CHAPTER 26

That night as I lay awake in bed trying to sort through my emotions, I thought I finally realized what the problem was. I felt powerless. I felt as if I didn't have control over my life any more. Instead of making decisions and going on adventures, I'd put everything on hold while I waited for Max to propose. What I needed to do was stop waiting!

I got so excited that I hopped out of bed and headed straight for my computer. I began researching my idea.

I soon discovered that I wasn't the only one with the idea. I even got into a few chat rooms filled with women who were planning, or had already succeeded in doing, what I thought might just be the solution to my problems.

The most difficult part was my patience growing thin as I waited for the sun to rise. As soon as it was up, I started making calls. I called a few places until I found a great deal.

"So, this is for a couples massage?"

"Yes, I'm sure you will both enjoy it."

"Do you have anything available for this afternoon?"

"Sure. You tell me when and I'll tell you where."

I knew that it had to be meant to be if it was flowing so easily. I booked the appointment for the afternoon. Then I sent Max a text with the address and the time.

Please be there. I can't wait to spend some time with you.

He didn't text back right away, but I knew it was still very early. He might not have even seen my text yet. As I waited for his response, I turned my attention back to my research. My heart fluttered with excitement at the idea. I no longer had that sick feeling that things were never going to move forward. Now I had the power to decide when and how they would move forward.

My phone chimed. It was a text from Max.

I'll be there. Looking forward to it. Love you.

I shrieked with happiness. There was no one in my apartment to hear it, but I imagined if there were, they would have shrieked with me. I felt like I had been completely transformed from the night before. I knew what I wanted and I was going to take it. I was so excited that I had to tell someone.

I called Stephanie.

"Hello?"

It sounded like I'd woken her up.

"I'm sorry, Stephanie, I know it's early, but I have to tell you something."

"What is it? Are you okay?"

"I'm great! I feel good again for the first time in a long time."

"Wait. Why?" She sounded more awake.

"Because I made a decision."

"A decision?"

"I made a plan." I could barely restrain my glee.

"What kind of plan?"

"All of this time I've been fretting about when Max would propose to me when all I really need to do is take matters into my own hands."

"What do you mean?"

"I mean that I'm going to propose to him!"

"What? No, you can't do that!"

"Oh, Stephanie, you can't be that old-fashioned. Women do it all the time now. Why should I have to wait for him to make the move? He's told me that he loves me, that he'll always love me, so why shouldn't I propose to him?"

"Samantha, I hear what you're saying, but I think that you're going to regret it."

"So you think he'll say no?" Her response hurt. I thought she would be as excited as I was. For her to act as if Max would turn me down just reminded me of the fact that Max could have his pick of women.

"Of course he won't say no. He loves you. But I think

that you should think this through. I mean, taking that opportunity away from a man is a huge deal."

"I hadn't really thought of it as taking the opportunity away."

"Think about it. When it comes to marriage, men really only get the proposal. The bride plans the ceremony and chooses the date in most cases, and she tends to be the focus of the wedding. The proposal is the only part that a groom gets entirely to himself as a way of declaring his love."

"It sounds like you've thought a lot about this," I said.

"I haven't really. But I've never enjoyed the proposals where women get on one knee. I mean, I understand that women should be just as free to propose, but give the man a chance!"

"I have given him a chance. He was supposed to propose on our anniversary, but he didn't."

"He was only supposed to because you thought he would. Max isn't going to propose until he's ready. I just feel like your asking him before he is will be rushing things."

"Wow, I really thought that you would have my back on this, Stephanie. I have to say I'm surprised."

"I always have your back. I just want you to have what you want. I think what you want is for Max to propose to you. Sure, you can pop the question and he will say yes, but won't you always wonder how he would have done it? How things might have happened if you'd been patient?"

I was annoyed. I could hear the honesty in Stephanie's voice. I knew she was trying to be a good friend, but what I really wanted was for her to cheer me on and think that it was a great idea. I didn't want any pesky logic messing up my plan.

"I'm tired of waiting. I want to move on to my life with Max, not just seeing Max here and there, but every morning—and every night. I mean, there's still a wedding to plan."

"I know what you're saying, but you need to take a breath and calm down. Max hasn't given you any reason to think that he's not going to propose."

"He hasn't given me any reason? How about our one-year anniversary coming and going?"

"Samantha, you thought he was going to propose then, but maybe he just wants to surprise you. Maybe he wants to do it when you won't expect it."

"I have it all planned out. It will be perfect. I'll make it memorable."

"But you will always remember having to do it. I know you, Samantha. A part of you will still doubt. You will start torturing yourself. You will wonder if Max would have asked you, how he would have asked you, whether he resents you for asking. I mean, there are so many things that could go wrong."

"Stephanie, if you think it's a terrible idea, just tell me

that. You don't have to beat around the bush about it."

"I'm just playing devil's advocate. Sometimes I get all wound up about something and don't think it through."

"Alright, alright. I'll think about it." I frowned.

CHAPTER 27

I hung up the phone and began to pace. I'd planned to go down to the jewelry shop and pick Max out a ring. I wanted to have something to give him when I asked him to marry me. But the more I thought about it, the more I realized that it might not be the best way to start things out with us.

I hadn't even really considered the possibility that he could say no. I just wanted it to be done. I wanted to move things forward. But would I be moving them backward instead? Was it possible that I could cause irreparable damage?

All morning I'd been so certain of what I wanted to do, and now all of that was out the window again. Stephanie hadn't reacted the way I expected she would at all. Now I was feeling a bit nervous that there could be consequences to my being the one to propose.

I decided that I would still go through with the couples massage. Max and I needed a day together to reconnect, no matter how it ended. I would wait until after to decide whether or not I would go through with the proposal. Even though Stephanie had made some good points, I wasn't ready to give up on the idea yet.

I was sure it was what Zara—one of my favorite characters from my new book series—would do. Life wasn't about waiting, it was about seizing the day.

Of course all of this would be a surprise to Max. I left the apartment to meet him. He only had an address. He had no idea what was in store for him.

When I reached the small office space, Max waved to me from the front door.

"Hi, gorgeous. Ready to tell me what this is about?"

"You'll see." I smiled at him. "I know you've been wanting some attention and I've had my nose buried in my computer, so I planned a special surprise for us."

"I like the sound of that." Max gave me a quick kiss. "But this is where it is?"

"Yes, let's go in."

I opened the door and we stepped into the heady scent of vanilla candles. The lights were dim. Despite the fact that we were in the middle of the city, the sounds of the rain forest surrounded us. On the floor was a thick massage mat along with a basket of an assortment of oils.

"Oh wow, this is a surprise." Max grinned.

I noticed there was only one mat. I thought couples massage meant we were massaged at the same time.

"Hello?" I called out. I wondered if the massage had been so cheap because I only ordered a single massage by mistake. I hoped I could straighten things out before my plan for the day got ruined.

"Is someone supposed to be here?" Max looked around the room. "I don't think anyone else is here."

Max was right. The office space was small. The only door led to a tiny bathroom. There was nowhere for anyone to be hiding. My aggravation started to increase. I wanted everything to be special. Instead it was a disaster.

"Just give me a second Max. I'm sorry." I pulled out my phone and dialed the number I had called to order the massage.

"Hello?"

"Hello, this is Samantha. I ordered a couple's massage—for right now." I stumbled over my words as I became more and more flustered.

"Hi, Samantha. Is there a problem?"

"Uh, yes."

"Is the music on? Did you find the basket?"

"Well, yes, and yes, but where are you?"

"Me?"

"Yes, you."

"Oh, Samantha, I'm not included." She laughed. "That's a different kind of service."

"I'm sorry, what?" Now, not only was I flustered, I was confused.

"Oh, I'm sorry. I think you've misunderstood."

"What did I misunderstand?"

"The couple's massage doesn't come with a masseuse.

I provide the space, set the mood, and provide the supplies. Then you massage each other."

"That's nonsense. I've never heard of anything like this."

"I understand. It's a new concept. So far everyone who has tried it has really enjoyed it. I think if you give it a shot you might find that the intimacy is much more intense when you are the only two people in the room."

I hung up the phone before I could say anything that might get me arrested. I didn't order a couple's massage so that we could massage each other. We could have done that at home for free if we wanted to.

"I'm sorry, Max." I turned toward him only to discover that he was already sprawled out on the cushion.

"Sorry for what?" He lifted his head to look at me. "This is great."

"There's no masseuse. Apparently we're supposed to massage each other. I knew the price was too good to be true."

"Sammy, this is beautiful. I'd love the opportunity to massage you and to have you massage me. Why don't we just make the best of it?"

He sat up and pulled his shirt off. "Mind if I go first?"

I smiled at the sight of him. I didn't mind at all.

"Doesn't it seem weird, though?"

"Yes. It does." He stood up and dropped his pants.

"Max!"

"What?" He acted innocent as he dropped back down

on the mat.

"Are you sure you want to do this?" I looked down at him sprawled across the mat in only his boxers. I couldn't help but see how beautiful he was. But more than that, he was at my whim. That made me feel powerful and nervous at the same time.

"Yes. I couldn't think of a better way to spend my afternoon." He laughed and gazed up at me. "Don't you want to massage me?"

"Yes. Yes, I do." I picked up one of the oils and sat down on the floor beside him. As I began rubbing along his arm, he smiled at me.

"I love your touch. It's so gentle and sensual at the same time."

"It is?"

"Yes. Even before we were together I loved the way you touched me. It would cause this strange spark inside me."

My eyes widened at his words. I had felt the same spark each time we touched. I began to relax. My hands ran smoothly from his arm and up over his shoulders.

"Oh, that feels good, thanks."

My heart fluttered. It felt wonderful to know that I was doing something he enjoyed.

CHAPTER 28

I found myself getting more and more comfortable. I shifted my body so that I was straddling Max. It was something I never would have done in the past, as I would tell myself that I would crush him. Under my fingertips, I could feel his every muscle and the warmth of his skin. I knew that he was much stronger than I gave him credit for.

"You're so tense here." I rolled the heel of my palm along the curve of his shoulder.

"I've been a little stressed." He spoke so quietly that I almost missed his words.

"Because of me?"

"Because I wanted to know what was going on with you. I still do." He turned his head enough to look up at me. "Are you ready to talk to me about it yet?"

"Everything's fine." I felt his muscles twitch beneath my touch. I realized that my vague response had a direct impact on him. "I mean, you know me, Max. I just always have all of these insecurities."

"That's not true. You've dealt with so many of those

over the past year. We all have some, Sammy. It's okay to be afraid. Just tell me if that's what it is."

I smiled and ran my hands down along the slope of his back. I was dazzled by him. I had never felt so attracted to a man before.

"Maybe I am a little." In the candlelight, the soft music, and with his skin gliding under my fingers, I felt safer speaking the truth. "I'm just scared that you're going to wake up and realize that you made a mistake one day."

Max turned over under me. It was a little surprising, to say the least. He slid his hands up over my hips to keep me from toppling over.

"Sammy, if that's what all of this is about then tell me how I could prove to you that's not going to happen. Just tell me, and whatever it is, I'll do it."

I stared at him for a moment. The words were on the tip of my tongue. I could propose right then in the candlelight. He couldn't get away. I had him pinned against the mat. Then I remembered what Stephanie had said about taking away his moment.

"I just need to know it's forever." I frowned. "I know that's not fair to you—that there's no way for you to prove that to me. But that's the truth."

"Okay, I think it's your turn."

I expected an argument. I expected him to try to prove to me that it would be forever. Instead, it seemed as if he was more interested in getting me on the mat. I wondered if I'd pushed him too far by asking him for forever. I started to lie down on the mat.

"Aren't you going to take your shirt off? I took mine off."

"I don't know. Do you think I should?"

He didn't answer. He just lifted it off for me. It was odd to be undressing in a strange place. But with Max there I felt better about it.

I sprawled out across the mat. I didn't take my bra off. But once Max straddled me he released the clasp so that he could rub oil on my back. I tensed at first. It was unusual for me to not try to cover up when someone was looking at me.

As I felt his weight against my hips and the cool air against my bare skin, I suddenly understood what it was to be vulnerable. I had exposed my heart to him, and I had exposed my body to him. His fingertips roamed across my skin as if they were trying to map out every freckle, every dimple, every imperfection that I'd memorized. I felt fully known by Max as he took his time with the massage.

My body began to relax. My mind followed suit. All of a sudden I felt tears in my eyes. They weren't tears of sorrow, but tears of closeness. I felt more connected with Max than I had since that first day we kissed.

It was me that had put up the wall when our relationship moved from friendship to romance, not Max. It was me that had started to fill the role of girlfriend, rather than just being who I was.

"Oh, Max, I'm so sorry."

"Sh. You have nothing to be sorry for." His voice was as soft as the glow of the candles.

"Yes, I do. You're right. I have been hiding from you."

His fingers kneaded deeper against my lower back. "You might have tried, but you can't hide from me, Sammy."

"I tried to be your girlfriend, instead of just being me."

"I know." He rubbed his hands up along my back all the way to my shoulders and down again. I shuddered with euphoria at the sensation he created. It was more powerful than anything I'd ever felt. "But I still saw you. I never wanted anyone or anything but you, Sammy. I can't make you see that. You have to find a way to trust me."

"I do trust you, Max. I do."

He smiled and leaned down to kiss the top of my head. "Then trust us, Sammy. Trust what we have now and what we will always have."

All of my desire to propose to him faded. I didn't want to ask him. I never had. I wanted him to ask me. But I'd been afraid that he wouldn't.

After feeling the way he caressed my body and hearing the love in his voice, I knew that he would. Maybe it didn't make sense to me—why Max would want me instead of any other woman—but it didn't need to make sense. It was the truth.

I turned over under him and we spent the remainder of our session snuggled up on the mat.

CHAPTER 29

After our couple's massage, Max and I went out to dinner. I didn't care that I was still glistening with oil. Neither did he. I could talk with ease to him again. We discussed where I was at with my book and a little bit about his work.

"Do you ever wish we could just take off together, Max?" The question fell from my lips without my taking the time to think about it.

"Where?"

"Anywhere. I mean, just explore the world. With my writing, now I can travel any time I like."

"My job is a little more limiting." He frowned. "But we could always work around that. I'd go anywhere with you."

"Europe?"

"Europe? That's a big one." He laughed. "Why not China?"

"China could work." I nodded. "I catch myself forgetting sometimes just how huge this world is and how many people there are that I'll never have the chance to meet. There are places on this planet that I bet no one has ever been to—at least no one that we know about. That's a great mystery, don't you think?"

"It is." He smiled and took my hand. "I'd love to explore the world with you. When do we start?"

There it was again, an opening for me to ask him to marry me. I could tell him that we could start right after he said yes. I held my breath and considered it. But the moment passed when I exhaled.

"That's up to you, Max. You're the one with the job, remember?" I winked at him.

"Don't remind me. It's been a little much to handle lately. Nothing but pressure."

"Really? Why haven't you told me about it?"

"You were busy." He shrugged. "Besides, there's nothing to do about it, really. I just have to adjust to the new policies."

"Max, I want you to tell me when something is stressing you out."

"I will—promise."

After the meal, Max drove me back to my car. We lingered there for a few moments and shared several kisses.

"Will you meet me for lunch tomorrow?" He met my eyes. "No excuses?"

"No excuses." I smiled. "I'll be there."

"Great." He squeezed my hand. I felt my spirits lift. It was wonderful to know that he wanted to be with me so often.

That night as I worked on my book I decided I needed a routine to keep me focused. Not just a routine for my writing, but for my exercises and spiritual endeavors as well. I planned to start the next morning. I would do some yoga when I woke up to get me going. I would work for a few hours. Then I would go for a run to the diner to meet Max.

I finally felt calm as I went to bed that night. I was no longer aching for Max to propose. I knew that he would when he was ready. I was no longer tormenting myself with my own flaws. I knew that Max loved me as I was and for who I was—and that I could love me too, if I tried.

When I woke up the next morning I felt better than ever. I went through the process of my yoga DVD—this time without earbuds.

Then I sent a text to Stephanie.

Thanks for talking me down from the ledge. I didn't go through with my plan. I'm really glad I listened to you.

Trust me, Samantha, when the time is right, it will work out.

I took her words as inspiration. I'd been trying to force something that wasn't meant to be forced.

After getting some work done on the book, I took the time to change into my most comfortable sweatsuit. Sure, it was threadbare and saggy in the wrong places, but it was also my favorite outfit to run in. The diner was only a few blocks away, so it wasn't like I was running a marathon.

As I took off running for the diner, I savored the feel of the wind against my face. I hadn't realized how much I missed that sensation of freedom. I'd been neglecting the parts of me that needed my attention, while focusing on something that I had no control over.

I ran fast. I wanted to leave behind all of my insecurities, all of my worries, and get to the real me—the Samantha that was far too used to being hidden away.

By the time I reached the diner my chest was tight and my legs ached. I could feel the sweat trickling down my back. The run had done me good in many ways, but I might have pushed myself a little too hard. I felt dizzy and exhausted.

I paused outside the diner and pulled out my phone. I thought about texting Max to cancel. I knew he wouldn't care about my workout gear or my sweat, but all I wanted to do was crawl into bed. Before I could type out a text, Max walked up to me from the other end of the sidewalk.

"Sammy, you look beautiful." He kissed my cheek.

"If you say so." I grinned at him. I knew that when I caught a glimpse of Max covered in sweat from moving things, working out, or playing on the beach, I did find his glistening body attractive. Maybe he thought the same thing about my sweat-dampened hair and flushed cheeks.

"I'm starving. Are you ready to eat?"

"Absolutely."

He held the door open for me and we stepped inside.

CHAPTER 30

The lunchtime crowd was pretty slim. Our usual waitress smiled at us as we entered. She pointed to our usual table. I noticed that there was someone sitting close to our table, even though the rest of the diner was pretty empty.

"Should we sit somewhere else?" I frowned. I didn't want to offend anyone with my sweaty state.

"No, this table is good." Max steered me to it.

Once we were settled he picked up the menu. I sat back and watched him for a moment. At any other restaurant his perusing the menu would not have been strange. But we had been to the diner so many times that we didn't even need menus.

"What can I get you guys today?"

Mandy, the waitress, grinned at us. I smiled back. It always brightened my dining experience when the waiter or waitress was friendly.

"My usual. I think Max is looking for something new, though."

"Nope, just a cheeseburger." He handed her his menu.

I shook my head and took a sip of the water that Mandy left behind on the table.

"One of the hardest things I've ever had to do was wait this long to do this…" Max smiled at me. His hands fluttered nervously. "But I wanted it to be on this exact date, and I couldn't imagine doing it any other way."

I had no idea what he meant. What was so special about today? I watched as he stood up from the table.

"Max?"

He smiled again. He reached out and took my hand. I could feel that his palm was sweating a little. As he kneeled down, our favorite song began to play. It was as if the universe conspired to make that moment special— or perhaps it was Mandy.

I could barely take a breath, as I was afraid to get my hopes up. He couldn't be, could he? With me dressed like I was, with my hair a mess, with my heart leaping out of my chest? Don't do it, Sammy, I warned myself. Don't get your hopes up. This is just like the last two times.

"Sammy, you are the most important person in the world to me. I close my eyes, and I see your smile. I can't think of a single good memory since college that hasn't involved you. My only regret is that it took me so long to discover my true feelings for you. That's why today is special. Because two years ago today, we sat at this table, and even though I was here with Stephanie, I looked into your eyes and I knew. It finally dawned on me that I was madly, deeply, and eternally in love with you."

I gasped. I hadn't even remembered that day. I knew that it had happened, but I had no idea that Max's feelings had changed so suddenly.

"Oh, Max." I smiled at him with tears in my eyes.

"So I chose today, to show you just how much I want you to be a permanent part of my life. You've been a part of my past and my present, and I want to know that you will always be a part of my future." He reached into his pocket.

It's just a necklace, Samantha. Don't think it's a ring. It's not a ring. It's not a ring.

He pulled out a black jewelry box. He flipped the lid open and looked up at me.

"It's a ring!" I didn't expect those words to pop out of my mouth. A few people around us laughed, and so did Max.

"It's your ring, Sammy. Will you marry me?"

Hearing those words caused my head to spin. I paused long enough to discern with certainty whether I was in a dream or not. Max squeezed my hand and pulled me out of my trance.

"Yes! Yes, I will! A million times I will!"

"No, only once." He grinned and plucked the ring out of the box. "Because now that we've finally found our way into each other's hearts, I know, I trust, I am certain, that we will never part ways again."

I stared down at the sparkling diamond that glistened up at me. I didn't notice its cut or clarity. I didn't notice the setting. I only saw that it fit perfectly.

"Max, I love you!" I stood up in the same moment that he did, and we narrowly avoided knocking heads.

He grabbed my face gently and pulled my lips to his for a long passionate kiss. I was distantly aware that people were applauding and cheering around us. Someone was also taking pictures.

I knew then that Max had planned all of this. He had taken the time to make sure that it was perfect and meaningful. My heart felt as if it would burst with joy.

Only a year before I'd believed that I would never even kiss Max. Now everything had changed.

Now when I looked into his eyes, I didn't see my best friend who would never return my love. I saw Max, my fiancée—Max, my future husband—Max, the love of my life.

A NOTE FROM THE AUTHOR

Fictional character, Samantha Bradford and the Single Wide Female books are written for every woman out there who has struggled with their weight, self-esteem and any number of issues that we all face as we work to become the best versions of ourselves that we can be.

These books are meant to be light-hearted and fun, with the hope that they will also inspire you to make your own "bucket list" of sorts—and to REALLY live your life to the fullest, loving yourself completely as you do so.

Lillianna loves to hear from her readers and can be contacted via her website where you can also download a complimentary book.

LilliannaBlake.com

ALL TITLES BY LILLIANNA BLAKE

http://Amazon.com/author/lilliannablake
*Check the author page for current list of titles

Single Wide Female in Love
#1 The Date
#2 The Girlfriend
#3 The Fiancée
#4 The Wife

Single Wide Female: The Bucket List
#1 Learn Pole Dancing
#2 Start a Blog
#3 Learn to Cook
#4 Create a Masterpiece
#5 Run a Marathon
#6 Go Skinny Dipping
#7 Start Online Dating
#8 Learn Yoga
#9 Be a Mentor
#10 Crash a Wedding
#11 Be a Movie Extra
#12 Join a Writing Group
#13 Enjoy a Spa Day
#14 Donate Blood
#15 Learn Poker
#16 Get a Tattoo

#17 Host a Dinner Party
#18 Publish a Book
#19 Walk Across Hot Coals
#20 Learn to Swim
#21 Learn to Meditate
#22 Quit My Job
#23 Learn to Salsa
#24 Fall in Love

Other Single Wide Female Titles
My Valentine's Day
St. Paddy's Day Disaster
A Bunny Tale
Sammy's Christmas List

Becoming Zara
*how the B.I.G. Girls Club came to be

B.I.G. Girls Club
The Rockstar's Girlfriend
The Former Model

Visit the author website at LilliannaBlake.com to get on the notification list for new releases and to receive a complimentary book to learn what inspired Sammy to begin her bucket list.